LIPSTICK KISS

THE TURNERS OF COPPER ISLAND
BOOK 3

GRACE HARPER

GRACE HARPER

LIPSTICK KISS

By

Grace Harper

The Turners of Copper Island
Book #3

Lipstick Kiss by Grace Harper
Copyright © Grace Harper 2023
The right of Grace Harper to be identified as the author of this book has been asserted by the Copyrights, Designs, and Patents Act 1988. Accordingly, copying this manuscript, in whole or in part, is strictly prohibited without the author and her publisher's written permission. It licenses this book for your personal enjoyment only. This book may not be re-sold or given away to other people. If you would like to share this book with another person, please purchase an additional copy for each recipient. If you're reading this book and did not buy it or have not purchased it for your use only, please return it and purchase your own copy. Thank you for respecting the hard work of this author.
All sexually active characters in this work are 18 years of age or older.
This is a work of fiction. Names, characters, places, and incidents are solely the product of the author's imagination and/or are used fictitiously, though reference may be made to actual historical events or existing locations. Any resemblance to real persons, living or dead, business establishments, events, or locales is entirely coincidental.

Published by GAVON Publishing, 2023
All rights reserved

❊ Created with Vellum

1

Freya

"I'm not speaking to you," Freya said, turning her back on her best friend.

Laughing heartily, Heidi came around the other side of the sofa in Freya's front room and sat next to her.

"What is it today that irks you, babe?" Heidi asked, tugging on Freya's pussy bow on her blouse.

Freya shifted up the sofa and sniffed the air like she'd smelled something foul. This made Heidi laugh harder.

"You don't live next door anymore. You buggered off and got married and left me all alone to fend for myself. You took the chef with you, too."

"He is my husband," Heidi said, holding her hand out to admire her engagement ring and wedding band. They shone under the overhead light. Freya felt a pang of jealousy that Heidi had married a Turner. Once upon a time, Freya wanted to marry a Turner, not any Turner, but Luke Turner, her best friend. However, after his last two visits home, it was clear he wasn't interested in her other than friendship.

Folding her arms, she drummed her fingers on her elbow. "Still mean."

"Are you missing his cooking or me?"

"Both," Freya whined.

Heidi tapped the toes of her clogs together, then swivelled to the side to face Freya. "Well, you need to get over it, as I have an awesome thing to show you," Heidi said, holding up her hands like she was a mine artist.

That got Freya's attention. "More awesome than the rock I have stashed in my sock drawer?"

Heidi frowned, excellent news forgotten momentarily. "I forgot I gave that to you. Jason can't stand seeing it and won't return it to Cynthia. Unfortunately, none of the siblings are talking to their aunt, so I can't get Archer to do it. Maybe Luke will take it to his aunt. Can you keep it a while longer until we know what to do with it?"

"Of course," Freya readily agreed. That meant she could try it on again before she had to part ways with the biggest diamond she'd ever seen. "What awesomeness do you have to show me?"

Heidi stood and downed the last of the coffee in her mug and walked to the kitchen attached to the living room. "Can you be at Edward Hall for six tomorrow morning?" she called out after Freya heard the water go on and off.

"O'clock?" Freya said, aghast.

Heidi chuckled on her way back into the living room.

Freya loved her tiny house. She could walk from the kitchen through the opening with no door into her living room and then past the open staircase to her front door in fifteen steps. It was perfect for lazy Saturday mornings. If she positioned her body just right on the sofa, she could watch TV and be nosey looking out of the window to see who was wandering past. Her front door opened straight onto the street.

"Yeah, what else? It will only take ten minutes. Plenty of time to go to the kitchens for my husband to make you breakfast before you have to teach teenagers."

Heidi shuddered at her words, and Freya laughed.

"Teenagers are cool. I'd rather teach them than look at women's vaginas all day," Freya quipped and scrunched up her face.

"Meh, seen one, seen them all. Anyway, is that a yes?"

"Only if Jason makes me a bacon bap with his home-made tomato sauce. I want a white floury bap, large, with proper butter. I'll bring my travel mug for the expensive coffee, I know he has stashed in the lockable store room."

Heidi laughed hard and dragged her friend into a hug. "I'll be sure to let him know. You won't regret it, I promise."

Heidi kissed her cheek, and Freya watched her with squinty eyes as she picked up her OBGYN bag, straightened her nurse's top, and left. Freya waited until she passed the window before she finished her coffee and looked around to see where her school bag was.

Freya loved that her best friend was doing her dream job. They were rocking it like they'd always planned.

Freya wasn't exaggerating when she felt lonely. They'd always lived near each other. Copper Island was small, but it was still a buggy ride up to the cottages where Jason and Heidi lived. Plus, her best friend was only three months married, and she didn't want to be a third wheel.

Freya sipped her second coffee while pouring her third into a travel mug. She loved teaching, but she needed caffeine to fuel her enthusiasm.

Thankfully, it was Friday. One more day to get through,

and Luke would be home for good. She'd missed him so much over the last nine years. She sent him letters, and he sent her postcards, letters, and parcels, but it wasn't the same as having him back on the island.

Over the past year, he'd come back for odd days here and there, and they spent as much as he could mess about or drinking in the pub. But, from tomorrow onwards, he would be back permanently, and Freya wouldn't be lonely anymore.

Hefting her school bag over her shoulder, she grabbed her keys from the hook and left her home, making sure the door was secured. Climbing the wide shallow steps to the school, she sighed and straightened her back. Through the two sets of glass doors with leaded windows was Mr Morris, the head teacher at Copper Island High School. Dudley Morris was elderly in years, but not in body. He was quick as a whippet, smart as a tack and mean as a snake. Vicious barbed attacks that were non-specific enough that Freya couldn't go to the school board. Not that she would. Cynthia Turner headed it up. She didn't see the point of complaining. Why Mr Morris targeted her was lost on her.

Teachers weren't begging to work at the school. They were a small island, so they didn't need many teachers, but required enough to cover classes. Freya was the most recent hire into the school, so Mr Morris had decided she took the slack. It didn't matter that she got the job years ago. Good for her experience, he said. This meant any teacher who needed a class covering when Freya wasn't teaching was down to her if she didn't have a class of her own. Since Christmas, it wasn't so bad she wasn't at home, as her best friend Heidi was either helping mums bring their little ones into the world, or she was enjoying being a newlywed and hid away in her cottage up at the Turner estate.

After school, drinks on a Friday had been dropped, and Saturday mornings watching TV slouched on the sofa while they recovered from their hangovers was a thing of the past. When Mr Morris insisted that she covered the evening classes, it forced her to mark books late at night or on weekends.

Fortunately, she didn't have a relationship to nurture because the man wouldn't have stuck around with the few hours she had spare a week she wasn't sleeping.

But then, that was another reason Mr Morris gave her. She was single, and the other teachers were married with children. The more Freya questioned his logic, the more he piled on her, so Freya kept quiet and accepted what he had dished out. She'd gone through the entire school timetable and the after-school classes to brace her for the maximum amount of lessons she could cover on top of her own tasks.

It felt like Mr Morris had done the same.

"Ms Riley," Mr Morris said as she moved towards where he stood.

There was no option to avoid him as every student and teacher needed to pass that spot to turn left or right to get to the classrooms.

"Good morning, Mr Morris. How are you today?"

"Well, thank you," he replied, not looking at her.

She'd stopped when he greeted her, but he said no more. Then, shoving the heavy bag further along her shoulder as it started slipping down, she strode away.

"Uh, Ms Riley," Mr Morris called out.

Freya stopped, dropped her chin to her chest and wished she'd copied the other teachers who wore trainers to work and changed into heels when they arrived. Then, lifting her chin, she pivoted on the spot, narrowly missing a student as her book bag swung out. The kid deftly swerved out of the way and continued down the corridor.

Walking back to where Mr Morris stood, Freya plastered on a genial smile and waited. When he didn't speak for a few moments, preferring to squint at the students who were entering the school looking at their phones.

"Did you need me?" Freya asked.

"Not in the slightest," he said.

She tutted, thinking she'd walked right into that comment.

"I have put the evening class roster up in the staffroom. I thought I'd let you know, as you rarely go in there."

"I have a lot of classes, so I spend my lunch marking books or preparing lessons. I can't do that if I'm in the staff room."

"I don't care what your reasons are, Ms Riley. Check the roster and be sure to make a note of next week's extra duties."

Freya was about to protest after doing the evening classes for three months. The clocks had changed, which meant lighter evenings. Luke was coming home the next day, and she wanted to spend time with him. Plus, she was exhausted and needed to go to bed at a reasonable time for a month.

"Understood, Mr Morris. Is there anything else you need—want me to do?"

"I'll be sure to let you know if you are required to do anything further."

Mr Morris had perfected his condescending tone while she was a pupil at the school, but when it was aimed at her, there seemed to be extra venom. Taking his words as a dismissal, she turned back around, juggling her book bag, handbag, and lunch bag as she hurried out of his vocal range and into her classroom.

The bell wouldn't ring for registration for another thirty minutes. There was enough time to get herself sorted and put her game face on. Any chink in her armour, and the kids would seek it out and prod it until she blew. Seven years of teaching at the school proved she could survive anything the kids could throw at her, but she was battle weary. One more term to go, and then she had six glorious weeks of doing nothing.

THE FOLLOWING morning at the crack of dawn, she sleepily drove the buggy up to Edward Hall. Freya parked at the end of the row of cottages and hoofed it to the kitchens in the depths of the mansion. Putting a shoulder to the door to the back entrance, she entered the spotless kitchens and spied Jason and her best friend kissing up against the wall. They were oblivious to her entry.

"Don't you two ever stop?" Freya called out, unwinding her scarf.

Heidi pulled away from Jason with a grin, pecked his lips, and shuffled out of his embrace. Jason had a stupid look on his face as he straightened his chef whites and then plucked his hat out of his pocket and put it on his head.

"Don't take your scarf off, lady. We're going," Heidi barked out.

Winding the long blue wool scarf around her neck, she fixed her gaze on Heidi, who was shoving on her coat.

"But what about my bacon bap? You promised," Freya whined.

"It will be ready by the time you get back," Jason said

from the other side of the vast expanse of kitchens. "Just getting the supplies now. Brown sauce, wasn't it?"

"You know it's ketchup, matey," Freya replied, attempting to give him an evil stare, but he kept his back to her as he yanked open the industrial walk-in fridge.

Heidi came to her side, fastening her grey hip-length coat. She was fresh as a daisy at five to six in the morning. Freya grumbled internally at how fantastic she looked.

Giving Freya a broad smile, she hooked her arm through hers. "Come on, grouchy. I have something that will cheer you up. More than a bacon bap and Luke's return."

"What the hell have you got planned? A private viewing of Magic Mike's west end show?"

Heidi laughed, tightening her arm through Freya's and said, "Better. Much better."

Freya let her coat flap open as she hurried along the path outside Edward Hall, following Heidi. They skirted the back and dashed up the shallow wide steps to a large stone verandah overlooking the lawns. Archer had planned for brides to stand on the balcony and throw their bouquets over the balustrade to the waiting singles underneath to catch. The verandah was large enough to fit fifty people with a five-piece orchestra. The doors to the ballroom were closed with the curtains drawn. It wasn't until she was halfway across the stone slabs that she saw a dozen men in long shorts and vest tops doing pushups in the grass. A lone man was pacing and shouting. By the time Freya reached the balustrade to look over, she had needed to prop herself up. Twelve fit, sweaty men worked out on the lawn.

"Good Lord, who the hell are they?" Freya whispered.

"We have them as guests for a while. They're here to train in the water but warm up on the grass first," Heidi said, nudging Freya's side with her elbow.

Freya looked to her best friend open-mouthed and then back at the men. They were finishing up and standing with their hands on their hips. All of them.

"Holy hotness, Heidi. They do this every morning?"

"Yep."

"At six?"

"Yep."

"I'll be popping by. Tomorrow I'll bring a blanket and a chair," Freya said.

Heidi laughed, which caught the attention of one of the men. He looked up at Freya, gave her a wink, and pulled off his vest. Freya clutched Heidi's arm like she was about to have the vapours and stared at the man's naked torso.

"I've never in my life seen abs like his," she whispered.

"Luke has gotta look like that, surely?" Heidi responded.

"I've never seen Luke naked or even topless in the last ten years. Anyway, why would I want to see Luke when there are all these men to gawp at," Freya said, spreading her arms wide.

One by one, the men stripped off their shorts and peeled off their vests, throwing them in a pile. Each man wore a version of swim shorts that were very short and very tight fitting. They moved their arms, jumped up, and stretched while the instructor was bellowing at them. Freya was too far away to hear what he said, but she knew he was barking orders. Then, as a unit, they ran off across the lawn towards the top of the path that led down to the beach and was gone.

"Where'd they go?" she said, whimpering. "The beautiful men have gone."

Freya reached out her hand to touch them in her mind.

"They'll be back tomorrow, babe. Let's eat, and then you can go back to bed for a nap."

"All right. But I am serious about coming back tomorrow. Do you have their names and marital status?" she asked.

Heidi laughed and leaned in to kiss her cheek.

"No, sadly not. Archer has a company name, and the rest is need to know. They're some elite group of men who want private land to do whatever they're preparing for that requires them to have expert sea training," Heidi said.

"They have to be private hire mercenaries. It can't be ex-marines, as they'd have the training. Navy, probably too. Maybe they're a secret branch of the army. MI6 or is it MI5?" Freya babbled, ticking each one off on her fingers.

"Honestly, Freya, you can't interrogate them. We are strictly looking only, no contact."

"Seriously, no touching?"

"Especially no touching."

"Well, that's a bummer," Freya said.

"For me, no, as I have Jason, but for you, yes. It's the biggest tease, but at least you can watch."

"Feels a bit pervy," Freya said, wrinkling her nose. "Maybe I can take one of the rooms upstairs and watch from the window?"

"Nope, not allowed in. Kitchens are the only place we're allowed to go."

"Definitely, Army," Freya said, nodding. "Okay, food. Then maybe I might come back and see if they want me to spot them."

Heidi laughed and dragged her away from the verandah.

2
___

Luke

It was too early in the morning to deal with a bunch of bullies who thought five-on-one was a fair fight.

Luke had come off the first boat to cross to Copper Island with his duffle bag. Walking along the quayside, he saw two fishermen who ignored his nods.

"Aunt Cynthia, making friends again, I see," he muttered.

He had a short walk to the high street before taking the private path to the Turner estate. He looked down the main street with the shops and saw five boys shoving another kid who wasn't trying to defend himself or run away. He stood there, taking it. Then, dropping his duffle bag, Luke ran towards them. When he got to their scuffle, he saw they were young teens. He recognised the one being shoved. It was Ralph's kid, Kenny.

"Kenny, back away, stand over there, and you lot," he

said, pointing at the group of five kids he'd put at fourteen, "come over here."

It was too early for them to be up. They were teenagers. All of them should be in bed and not get up until midday.

"What's going on?" Luke said to the five boys, but then got distracted.

Out of the corner of his eye, he could see Kenny edge away.

"You stay still," he said to him.

The kid was so scared he froze mid-stride and stood legs apart outside the newsagents.

Luke turned back to the kids and glared at them. "Who is the leader?"

Four eyes looked at the boy in the middle, who stared at Luke like he was Lord of everything.

"You lead this chicken shit bunch of losers?" Luke asked.

"We're not losers," he called back, chin lifted, his lips scrunched together.

"You think five to one is brave?" Luke bellowed.

The shopkeeper came out of the newsagents. He nodded to Luke and then went back inside. Luke spotted Lucy come out of the greengrocers with a crate of apples.

"Hey, Luke. Good to see you home," she called out.

At least one person was happy to see him back that wasn't blood.

Turning back to the lead punk, he nodded for him to explain, crossing his arms.

"He hasn't paid up this week. He knows his money is due on a Friday. It's now Saturday, and he hasn't paid."

Luke didn't think this happened any more in schools. What concerned him was that these kids weren't hiding what they were doing.

"What does he owe you money for?"

"Protection."

"For what?" Luke said, laughing.

"Not getting picked on."

"By whom?"

"Ooohh, fancy," one of the kids said. "Whom," he sang.

"Shut it," Luke said in a low tone, making the boy's bottom lip tremble.

Turning his attention back to the ring leader, he said, "What will his money buy him?"

"Our protection."

"So you want him to pay you to not beat him up, is that right?"

"Yeah," he replied, proud of his racketeering.

"It's half six in the morning. You're dedicated. I'll give you that."

"Unless he's at school, this is the only place we can get to him. Kenny does a paper round. He spends most of his time at home with his dad or at the Turner estate."

"He's earning money, and you're stealing it? You're a pathetic waste of space. Are you going to charge me too?"

"No, the protection is just for the kids at school."

"All of them?"

"No, just the kids in the lower years."

"What happens if they don't pay?"

"They get a reminder with a boot and a fist to make payment," the kid said, attempting to look mean but not entirely pulling it off.

"I think I need to teach you a lesson. It goes like this. If you threaten anyone else from this moment, I will come and pay you a visit and give you a lasting reminder with my boot and my fist. Are we clear?"

The leader wasn't so brave looking at Luke.

"You know who I am?" Luke asked.

The boy shook his head.

"I'm Luke Turner. My aunt is on the board of governors for your school. You heard of Cynthia Turner?"

He nodded his head so fast that Luke thought it would rock off.

"Good. Hopefully, Cynthia Turner's name alone will make you think twice the next time you want to use extortion as a means to earn money."

Luke knew the kid didn't understand what extortion meant, but he didn't care. He'd had enough of keeping these kids in line. Instead, Luke wanted to get to his cottage, shower, and see Freya.

"Get lost," he said to the kids, and they sped off like their arses were on fire.

Luke turned to Kenny, who hadn't moved and was wide-eyed, looking at them disappearing.

"You all right, Kenny?"

"Yeah. Thanks, Mr Turner."

"It's Luke. You better get inside to do your paper round. Does your dad know about what's going on here?"

Kenny shook his head and looked like he didn't want Luke to tell Ralph about this incident.

"I'll keep my mouth shut, but if I see it happening again, I'll go with you to tell him."

Kenny's shoulders sagged like it was inevitable that would happen. Luke nodded for him to get to his job. He walked down the high street and lifted his duffle to make the journey home.

Home.

Luke didn't think he would ever consider Turner Hall his home. Still, there he was, fresh out of college with his qualification in pencil-pushing for event organising. He didn't want the job, but there wasn't much call for medics hosting weddings, so he'd chosen to organise the conference and banqueting business for Edward Hall. Stan Meyers and his daughter, Opaline, were still responsible for weddings. They dealt with the lead-up with the mother of the bride issues. Stan and Opaline looked after the sales side and then handed over the reins once everything was booked.

"Kill me now," he muttered as he trudged up the gravel path towards the Turner estate.

Walking along the path, he looked over the other side of the harbour to see if Freya's house was visible. There was a point on the trail where he could see right up her street. He stared when he reached that point, but there was no life on the quiet road. It was probably too early on a Saturday morning to be up. Unless you were bullies who wanted to terrorise a young kid. Luke made a mental note to ask Freya if she had taught them, especially the one leading the motley crew.

Strolling along the path in front of his sibling's cottages, he was surprised to see Jason and Heidi on the doorstep, letting themselves in.

"Hey," Luke called out and turned left to walk up their path.

"Dude, you're home. I thought you'd be in later," Jason said, striding down the path to meet him and wrapping him in a hug.

Heidi came too and gave him a cuddle and a kiss on the cheek.

"You've just missed Freya," Heidi said.

"What is she doing here so early, or did she stay over?" Luke asked as he followed them up the path and into their cottage.

He dropped his duffle just inside the door and toed off his shoes. Heidi had made the place so cosy he didn't want to mark anything with his dirty shoes from walking up from the harbour.

"She came to see our new guests. Once they headed to the sea to do their, well, whatever they needed to do," she said, waving her hand as she walked, "she declared it was time for a nap."

"It's half seven in the morning," Luke said.

"I know, but I made her come for six, or she would miss them," Heidi replied, heading to their kitchen. "You want some coffee?"

"Yeah, love one," Luke said, sitting at the kitchen island. "Who are the new guests at Edward Hall?"

"Some elite team, here for endurance training in the sea. We're not allowed to know anything about them. They've paid for everything upfront, and they're not doing anything illegal here, so we signed the NDA," Jason said, sitting next to him.

"Sounds intriguing," Luke said.

"They have bodies to die for," Heidi said with a sigh.

"Hey, I'm just here," Jason said, pressing his abs.

"Obviously, if you're into a rock-hard body. I like a little more softness," Heidi said.

"I don't know if I should be appeased or aggrieved," Jason muttered, still prodding his flat.

Heidi swept over and gave him a long kiss, and Luke had to look away. She was teasing Jason to get a reaction, and it was sweet how they got over what could have made other couples get pissed off.

"Is Freya going back to her place?" Luke asked.

"Yeah, not that she's happy about that, with my place empty. She's still grumpy I've moved into the cottage with Jason."

"You're married, though. She'd have to let you go at

some stage. It's not like you've moved off the island," Luke said.

"It is weird for me too. We've always lived next door to each other. I used to see Freya every day. I know it's just a five-minute buggy ride away, but we can go two days in a row without talking, and I miss my best friend."

Jason looked at me like I had the answer but didn't know how to solve best friend issues. My brothers and sister were my best friends.

"You'll work it out. Then, get into a new routine," Luke offered as a lame suggestion.

Jason laughed at my offering and poured Luke a coffee. They chatted for a while. Jason made him a breakfast burrito, and then Luke went to his cottage to shower. Heidi might have missed her best friend, but Freya was his best friend too, and he could guarantee he'd missed her more with the years he'd been away.

3

Freya

Freya wasn't sure when Luke would come to see her, but she was nervous. She had been besotted with him for so long, but now that he was coming home for good, Freya didn't know if they had a chance to move things along. She saw the looks his brothers gave them. Even Heidi and Erica gave her knowing looks, but Luke had been adamant that they were friends. Freya had dated while he was away. It wasn't like they'd promised to marry at thirty if they were still single. The last time they'd spent any real time together was before Luke went on the rigs nine years ago. Minds and bodies had changed a lot in that time. Luke was definitely a late bloomer. He was taller and broader the first time he came home from the rigs. Her best friend was no longer the beanpole he once was. He could easily have fitted in with the elite hotties she'd just salivated over.

She felt anxious, like she was going on a first date. Maybe she could be 21st century and ask him out.

Back in her small but cosy terraced house, Freya dashed upstairs to her sock drawer and pulled out the engagement ring box that Heidi had asked her to look after. It had been months ago her best friend had asked her to take care of it.

Every day Freya would bring it out and slip it on her engagement finger to see how it felt to have an extravagant piece of jewellery on her hand. The diamond sparkled under her side lamp. It was a little too small for her engagement finger, but she shoved it on, regardless. Tilting her hand this way and that, she admired the ring and wondered what would eventually come of it. For five minutes, she allowed herself to dream of getting a proposal with an obscene ring, and then she slipped it off and put it away.

Maybe from Luke.

Watching the men get hot and sweaty at six in the morning had turned her hormones riotous, hoping they might have their last night in the pub once their endurance week was over. She could admire them up close and personal. As she thought about tight abs and buns of steel, she went to pull off the ring, but it wouldn't budge. The more she yanked on her finger, the more swollen it became.

She ran downstairs and smothered her finger in washing up liquid, but it still wouldn't come off. Fretting and pacing, she wished she'd had ice in her freezer, but she rarely drank at her place. Heidi took care of the ice for their cocktails.

Heidi.

She would help her.

Freya grabbed her buggy keys off the hook by the door. She picked up her handbag from the side table and headed for the door. Unfortunately, when she swung it open, she wasn't looking up and walked straight into a wall of male muscle.

"Oomph," she muttered and then looked up. "Luke," she said, hugging him tight, throwing her arms around his neck.

"Freya," he said with a cool voice.

That was not the welcome she was used to when Luke came back to the island. Instead, this was a cold, stony voice that was clearly pissed off. She dropped her arms and stepped back onto her side of the threshold.

"What's wrong?" she asked as she righted her clothing and looked up at his face to see if his voice matched his expression.

It did.

"What in the fuck is that?" he barked, pointing at her hand.

He saw her hand for a split second before she threw her arms around him. How the hell did he see it so quickly? And why was he angry about it?

She went for the obvious. "An engagement ring."

His eyes widened like I was sassing him, and he had zero patience.

"I can see that. Someone proposed to you?"

Luke said it with so much disdain that she was hurt and immediately angry. How dare he be so shocked someone loved her enough to want to spend the rest of their lives with her? She was lovable, even if Mr Morris hated her existence.

So she lied.

Looping her handbag over her head, she tossed it on her sofa. There was no need to go and see Heidi now. She had a wedding to plan. And a fiancé to make up. She instantly went to the elite men on the lawn.

"Yes, why is that so hard to believe?"

"Because in all the letters you sent me, you never mentioned a boyfriend, let alone a fiancé. Also, you didn't have a ring on your finger the last time I was home a few months ago for Jason's wedding."

"It was a whirlwind affair," she offered, shoving her hand in her pocket, ashamed she was pleading her case. "I am lovable, you know," she said, huffing.

Freya lifted her hand to hook her keys on the nail hammered into the door frame. It paused halfway when Luke said, "You're entirely lovable. Who is he?"

Wait? What? She was thoroughly confused. But she had already told a lie. She needed to continue it. Freya hoped Luke had forgotten all her tells when she lied.

"No one you know," she said, hearing her snippiness.

Luke took a step forward, leaned his shoulder on the doorframe and folded his arms. He had an affectionate grin playing around his mouth as he spoke. Was she already busted?

"That's not hard, Freya. I haven't been back for any length of time in nine years. So I'd be hard-pressed to recognise more than ten people."

"It doesn't matter who he is, Luke Turner," she said.

Now she felt like she was talking like a ten-year-old.

"Yes, it fucking does, Peaches," he said, stepping closer, holding her face in his hands. "You're the closest thing I have to a best friend outside my siblings. No one will be good enough for you. So I want to meet the man who has proposed marriage."

Peaches. It had been years since she'd heard her nickname. Freya tilted her head to the side, snuggling against his palm, feeling warm everywhere.

"What happens if you don't approve?" she whispered.

"I'll talk you out of the marriage. Get some dirt on the guy and then convince you not to marry him."

He was immediate with his response. Was he being brotherly? Wherever this was coming from, he was possessive.

"You'd do that?"

"Fuck yeah, I would."

She'd never met this side of Luke. Possessive, protective and all fired up. His hands on her face heated her body in areas she wanted his mouth. Freya couldn't look away from his mouth. She was supposed to behave like an engaged woman.

"Are you going to let me go?" she said quietly, looking but not moving her head to see who was watching.

Luke stepped back onto the pavement and shoved his hands into his jeans pockets. "What are you up to?"

Trying to get a ring off my finger that cost half a quarter of a million quid.

"Not much. It's Saturday. What do you want to do?"

"I have a puzzle that needs solving," he said and grinned.

They'd spent most of their childhood trying to solve the Turner puzzles. It was what kept them amused until he went off to train as a medic and then onto the rigs.

"There is something unsolved?" she asked.

"Yeah, and I think it is going to reveal something massive. I feel it in my gut."

"You always say that, and it turns out to be something we could've found on the internet."

Luke gave her a mock shocked face and then pouted. "Where is your sense of adventure?"

"I'm not sixteen anymore," she replied.

"No, you're not," he replied, boring holes into the pocket where her hand was still stuffed.

"All right, when do we start?"

"Are you free on Monday?"

"I work, Luke. I'm a teacher. Did you forget?"

"Are they still in school?"

"Yeah, for like another three months."

"Shit, well, maybe we can do it in the evenings."

"Can't. The head teacher hates me, and I have four weeks of evening classes."

"What did you do to piss him off?"

"Exist, apparently. The downside of not being married is I get all the evening classes."

Luke looked thunderous, frown lines marring his handsome face.

"Is that why you're marrying Bozo?"

"He's a nice guy," she argued.

"Is that right?" he asked, giving her an insolent smile.

She was sure she was busted.

"Tonight, come up to Archer and Erica's place. They're having dinner to celebrate my return. Jason's cooking."

"Okay, what time?"

"Six."

"I'll be there," she said.

"I'll see you later," Luke said, not moving an inch. "Why won't you give me his name?"

"Because it is none of your business. I don't want you scaring him off."

"You know I like a puzzle and will stop at nothing to find out who he is. I bet he's a teacher."

She rolled her eyes and laughed nervously.

"See you at six, Luke. It's good to have you home at last."

Grinning, Luke took a step into the road, got a ring on a

bicycle bell for nearly toppling over a cyclist and then walked away.

She had ten hours to get the ring off her finger. Otherwise, Heidi and Jason would take one look at it and reveal she was a big fat liar.

TEN HOURS LATER, Heidi slid from the leather seat of the buggy with gloves on. She'd had to rummage through her mother's gloves to find a suitable pair that enabled her to hold a knife and fork. Or a glass. All her gloves were woolly, and she had to carry everything with two hands. Her mother had elegant gloves in every colour to match her winter coats. Freya imagined her mother could give Cynthia Turner a run for her money in the glove department.

She knocked on Archer and Erica's front door and kept her hands stuffed in the pockets of her trousers. She wore a loose-fitting pair of white trousers and a baggy blue blouse with cuffs that were too long. If need be, she could hide the ring under the cuffs. So long as she didn't raise her arm.

Erica opened the door and wrapped her in a big hug. "Come in. We're all out the back under the heat lamps. It's unusually warm for March, but I've switched them on just in case."

"Warm, do you think it's warm?" Freya asked with her best innocent-sounding voice.

"Don't you think so?"

Freya was almost home free when Erica spotted she was wearing gloves.

"Oh, are you cold? Let me get you a hoodie to wear over your blouse as we're outside."

"No, that's okay. I'll be fine."

I'll roast alive if I wear a hoodie.

"You're wearing gloves, honey."

Erica raced away from her up the staircase to her left and was back less than a minute later. Freya pulled on the hoodie, and to her joy, it had a front pouch pocket.

Even better than her pockets and cuffs idea.

"This is great, thank you."

Freya followed Erica through the kitchen and out into the open back patio area to the assembled group. Luke sat alone on one sofa. Heidi and Jason sat on another couch, and Archer sat on the oversized armchair. Erica went straight to her husband and sat on his lap.

Her only option was to sit next to Luke. She hadn't thought this through at all. He was going to mention the ring.

He absolutely would mention the ring when he saw her gloves.

Fuckit.

"Hey Freya, did you bring your fiancé tonight?" Luke asked as she sat down next to him.

Shit.

Four versions of *what the fuck* came her way. Heidi's was the one that cut the deepest. Freya didn't know where to look and had the urge to burst out laughing through sheer terror.

"I'll get you a drink while you show your closest friends your ring," Luke said.

It was almost like he knew she was lying through her teeth.

He kissed the top of her head as he passed her like he always did. At least some things stayed the same. Luke disappeared out of sight and into the kitchen. Luke knew what she drank, so there were no delaying tactics about what she could drink.

"What the hell?" Heidi hissed. "Show me the damn ring and then tell me why you kept this engagement from your best friend since birth," she yelled.

Freya could feel her shoulders rise so high that she had no neck left. Pulling her hands out, she was met with a laugh from Erica. "Is that why you're wearing gloves?"

"Yeah," she said, feeling sheepish.

Freya pulled off the glove on her left hand and waggled her finger.

"I know that ring," Erica said.

"Me too," Archer, Heidi and Jason said at the same time.

"It's stuck," Freya whispered. "I tried it on this morning, and it won't come off. I've tried everything. Then Luke rocks up unannounced, and he was so incredulous that someone wants to marry me, I pretended it was real."

"Who does he think you're marrying?" Heidi said through her snort laughing. She slapped her chest to stop choking.

"A teacher at school."

Heidi guffawed before she said, "But all the male teachers are already married."

"He doesn't know that," Freya hissed, checking over her shoulder to see if Luke was coming back.

"This is a movie waiting to be made," Erica said, leaning forward to get her wine glass.

"I got you a dirty martini. Took a while to find the olives," Luke said, coming out with a fancy glass with her cocktail.

"Thanks, Luke," Freya said, taking the drink from his hand.

"Did you show them?" he asked gleefully.

"Yep."

Freya took a long gulp of her drink. Her wide eyes scanned her friends to see them all stifling their laughter.

"I'm so glad I'm married," Freya heard Archer mutter, then kissed his wife on her neck.

"And did you spill a name?" Luke inquired.

"Nope. Thanks for letting the cat out of the bag before I could tell Heidi. Real gentlemanly."

"Aww, sorry, Peaches. I'm really happy for you. It's something to celebrate," Luke replied, then paused. "Don't you think?"

"Well, I'm sure Freya will introduce us to her future husband when she's good and ready. So stop cajoling her," Jason said.

"It's a hell of a ring," Heidi remarked. "Worthy of the Turner name."

Freya wanted to kick her best friend in the shin for her comment. If Freya wasn't in such a state of remembering all the lies so far, she'd laugh.

"Half a mil, I'd say," Erica commented. "Better never take it off, Freya, so you don't lose it."

"That's a great idea," Freya said, raising her glass. "Super idea."

Erica jiggled from her giggling on Archer's lap. She buried her face in his neck and stifled a howl.

Freya's heart stopped for a moment. She'd thought it was worth a quarter of a million but double? She was glad it was stuck because she wouldn't know what the hell she would do if she lost it.

"He must be filthy rich, Peaches. I bet he really knows how to treat you well," Luke said with so much smugness that she wanted to punch him for the first time.

"What's for dinner, Jason?" Freya asked.

4

Luke

Six o'clock on a Sunday morning was not a time to be awake. He couldn't shake the fact that Freya was getting married. They'd been friends forever. Explored the island, discovering all its mysteries. It was odd to think she'd bonded with someone else and not told him. Luke reasoned he'd been away for most of the last nine years, and what right he had that Freya would no longer be there whenever he knocked on her door.

Seeing the ring on her finger made him feel differently, like a curtain swooshed back, or a bulb changed to a higher wattage.

Luke didn't know what the difference was, but something shifted from thinking of Freya as the girl he grew up with to a woman who had a career and was seeing a man.

He did suspect she was making it up when he called on her the previous day, but when Heidi was so clearly hurt that she hadn't been told, it was evident it was true. Heidi wasn't that good an actress. He suspected Erica could pull it off but not Heidi.

Now he was tossing and turning all night, wanting to know who Freya had fallen in love with.

They'd agreed to meet at the back of his cottage at ten. Another four hours to wile away until he showed her what mystery they needed to uncover. He couldn't knock on Jason's door because he was still in the honeymoon phase. He couldn't knock on Archer's door because he didn't want to disturb Erica's sleep when she was six months pregnant with their first child.

Daisy was still on the mainland doing work experience at an accountant's office Erica had hooked her up with. It was the firm she used and pulled a few strings to get Daisy proper experience and jump the queue. The name Erica Taylor could sway her accountant to fit Daisy in for six months. I didn't want to call her as she was too far away.

Whenever Luke felt lonely when his siblings were busy, he always had Freya.

Moping in bed wasn't Luke's style. Instead, he showered and left his cottage to head to Edward Hall. Archer had told him that the elite team were doing endurance tests and would be working out. Luke wanted to see if he could work out who they were. Which branch of the military or special forces. Hell, he was plain curious and wanted to see what was so secretive they weren't allowed to know.

Luke rounded the corner of Edward Hall and jogged up the side stone steps to get up onto the wide verandah at the back of the hall. He stopped dead when he saw a lone figure slumped in a blow-up chair covered in a duvet. This didn't look like an elite fighter, and he would know that hair anywhere.

Walking as quietly as he could up to the back of the

chair, he observed the group of men strip off their shorts and vests and then run across the lawn to the path leading down to the beach. Freya hadn't moved in her seat after they disappeared from sight. He came to her side and crouched down when he saw she was fast asleep. Only her nose was peeking out. The hood of the jumper she had been wearing last night was pulled down over her eyes, and the duvet covered her completely.

Luke leaned in and kissed her nose.

They'd shared platonic kisses to the cheek, head and forehead for as long as he could remember. Now he thought if she belonged to another man, maybe he should stop touching her. He knew if Freya was his, he would be having a quiet conversation with any man who touched their lips to her, no matter how platonic it was.

If Freya was his? That sounded strange to say, but his heart warmed at the thought.

"Hey, sleepyhead," Luke said quietly.

Freya moaned, jolted her head from side to side and then pushed back the hood of her jumper with the hand that had the diamond. In the morning light, it sparkled. Did she really like an ostentatious ring like that?

She blinked a few times, looked across the lawns, and then at Luke.

"Hey, Luke. What are you doing here?"

"Well, I live just over there," he said, pointing to the cottages. "What are you doing here?"

Freya sat up, then fell to the side, like the blow-up chair was a bouncy castle. Luke watched her roll off and slowly stand, dropping the duvet to the side.

"Oh crap, I missed them," Freya crowed, flapping her arms to the side.

"Missed who?"

"The hot men," she said, pointing to the empty lawns.

"Why would you get up at dawn? Blow up a floating device, and drag a duvet to watch hot men exercise when you're engaged?"

He tilted her head as he watched the blood drain from her face. Freya wasn't a slouchy outfit kinda girl. Under her hoodie, she wore yellow loose-fitting cotton trousers and white lace-up plimsolls.

Freya's face went pale, and she looked to her ring, then the lawn and then back at Luke. Not a word came from her lips.

He was back to thinking she had made him up. Now he wanted to know why.

"Is your fiancé one of them?" Luke pointed to the lawns.

"I should go," Freya said, gathering her duvet under one arm and grabbing the inflatable with the other. "I'll see you at ten."

Luke laughed as she dragged everything across the flagstones and down the steps, including her body. He could hear the bumps of the chair as she trudged down and out of sight. He sauntered across to the low wall to watch her walk across the dew-soaked lawn towards the cottages where the buggy was probably parked. How she was going to get the inflatable home would be interesting. But then he could see her walk to Jason and Heidi's place and toss it into their back patio area.

Freya was lying. How much fun could he have making her squirm?

He spent the next few hours plotting to be evil to get her to admit she was making up a fiancé, and by the time ten o'clock rolled around, he was ready.

Luke had been sitting on the low wall in Archer's patio area, telling his brothers that he knew Freya was lying. They were sceptical.

"Tell me again why you think she's lying?" Jason asked.

"We tell each other everything," Luke replied confidently. "She wants me to believe she has found a man, dated him, fallen in love and now planning to marry the guy, and it's news to her best friend. Nope, don't buy it."

"And if you're wrong and she has been secretly dating someone because this town is so small, she would be under a microscope and would prefer to keep it all secret?"

"The thing about liars is they forget the lies they've told. I saw her three months ago. So she must have done all the schmoozing in the last two and a half months. Nope. Nope. Nope."

Archer and Jason stared at Luke like he'd lost his mind.

"Why do you care?" Archer asked.

Luke stood back and turned his cheek like he'd been slapped. "I don't."

"Yeah, you do. It's sweet. Listen, we need to focus on something else. You're back, and we need to have a handover of sorts. When will you be free of torturing Freya?" Archer asked.

"Two hours, maybe less if she's not talkative," Luke replied and slouched onto the wall at the rear of Archer's cottage.

Both his brothers lounged on the sofa with matching smirks. Jason looked at Archer, and Archer nodded back, grinning.

"What?" Luke asked, looking at one and then the other.

"Nothing, brother. I'll see you in a few hours."

"Hey," Freya said as she trudged along the grass to Luke's left.

"Hey, why are you coming from that direction?" Luke asked.

"Because, genius, you said to meet you at ten outside the back of your cottage. Here you are outside Archer's back door. Plus, why is the back of your cottage empty of anything to sit on. Even Jason's place has comfy chairs."

"I think you need a nap," Luke said.

"We're going. See you later," Jason said and sidled past Luke.

Archer followed. They both waved at Freya as they speed walked across the lawn to a minimum safe distance.

Pussies.

"I'm sorry, I'm pissy. I haven't had a lot of sleep. Lead on to the mystery puzzle for us to solve," Freya said.

"That's the spirit," Luke said, holding out his hand.

Freya looked at his hand and lifted hers to take it, but he dropped it.

"Ah, probably shouldn't do that now you're someone else's. Let's take a walk."

Freya frowned, looking at her hand to his and then back to hers.

"We can't hold hands? We always hold hands. We especially hold hands when we're on an adventure. And hey, you didn't kiss my head when I arrived."

"You belong to someone else now. It wouldn't be appropriate for me to touch you without speaking to him first. Ya know? Ask his permission, see how he feels about me holding your hand and kissing your temple. I feel bad enough that I kissed your nose to wake you up this morning."

"You did?"

"Yeah, you were asleep, so I don't think that counts."

Luke held back his laugh at the scowl Freya was throwing him.

"Fine, well, don't expect me to save you if you fall off the cliff like last time. You're on your own."

"Or," Luke said, elongating the word, giving her a side glance. "We could go see him, say hello, get to know each other."

Luke used his hands like he was shaking maracas, striding beside her as she took off across the lawn. He hadn't told her she was going in the wrong direction. He was having way too much fun pressing her irritated buttons. This was a new Freya.

"He's away," she said, stomping across the grass with her arms folded.

The short ponytail bobbed as she strode along. Luke zipped in front of her when they got to the fifth cottage in the row of houses his siblings lived in and held up his hands, careful not to touch her. They were at the same height as her breasts. He'd never paid that much attention to them before, but her deep breathing made his eyes zero in. Her white gipsy top showed a flash of cleavage. She was still in her yellow cotton trousers and white plimsolls.

"Where?" Luke asked.

"The mainland."

"Doing what?"

"Seeing friends."

"He has friends on the mainland?"

"I don't grill him with twenty questions like some people do. He's not here. You can't meet him. If I have my way, ever."

This time Luke burst out laughing. This was going to be fun. She was getting red in the face as her eyes darted about, no doubt thinking about what to make up about him.

"All right, fire breather, I'll stop with the questions for now. We need to head up to the graveyard."

"That's the other direction."

"I know," Luke said with enthusiasm.

"Yet here we are all the way over here." Freya sounded like she was ready to hit something.

"You were determined to come this way, and it's not like I could anchor onto your arm. That's against the rules."

"They're your rules, and they're stupid. You could have said words."

"I could've."

They strode across the lawns behind the lodges, through the gap in the twelve feet high hedges and across the lawns of Edward Hall. There wasn't an elite military type in sight. Luke was grateful because he already had to contend with Freya insisting she was engaged while ogling the men as they exercised.

Now came the dilemma. Did they cross the back of Turner Hall, passing the swimming pool and then up to the gravesite, or did they go the long way around, which would take them around the front of the manor house? Either way, he could get spotted by Cynthia.

"If we run, and she yells at us, we can ignore her," Freya said, grabbing his hand and crouching to make a run for it.

He curled his fingers around her hand and squeezed. Her fake fiancé would have to cope. He was touching her.

"All right. I hope you've still been working out because we're going to need to run fast."

"I'm good, Luke," she said, giving him a playful grin. "Fit as a fiddle, endurance to last all activities."

Was she flirting?

"I'm sure your fiancé is delighted."

Luke then got a grimace followed by a growl. She

dropped her hand and ran away across the perimeter of Turner Hall near the fence and trees overlooking the beach. He raced after her, following her laughter as she pulled the band out of her ponytail and shook her hair out. Freya then lengthened her stride. His legs were longer, and they were running side by side until they passed the swimming pool. They then passed the conservatory and then through the gap in the trees on the other side.

He didn't hear his aunt call out for him.

They were safe.

Slowing down to a jog and then a fast walk to then a stroll through the trees, he again took Freya's hand, and she didn't pull away. They caught their breath rather than spoke as they continued through the forest and out the other side.

The gravesite had all his ancestors buried in the same area. It looked like any gravesite, with lopsided gravestones, faded lettering and overgrown weeds. He had never known the site to be well kept. It seemed anyone dead was long forgotten. There were three exceptions. His father's plot, because one of his brothers took care of it and the other two he was about to reveal to Freya.

When they reached the two plain headstones, Luke stopped and hauled Freya around in a wide circle until she came to his side. He slung his arm around her neck and pointed to the gravestones with his other hand.

"What, the fuck, are these?" he clipped.

Freya stepped forward and out of his hold to take a closer look. When that didn't work, she dropped to her knees and leaned over the plot without kneeling on it.

"When did they arrive?" she asked.

"No idea. They weren't there when we buried Dad, but then I haven't been back for nine years. I didn't notice them until we came to salute Dad not long ago."

"Who do you think is buried here? The plots are well-tended. Someone must care about them. The headstones are a bit plain, though. Like someone doesn't want them noticed. Why are they far away from anyone else?"

"All great questions," Luke pointed out. "So you'll help me, right? To find out who they are?"

"Absolutely," Freya said, getting up and brushing off the dirt from her hands by clapping them together.

"We start Monday," he said.

"I told you I have to work, Luke, and so do you," she replied.

Shit, he'd forgotten about that.

"After work. I finish around four. What about you?"

"I have an evening class to teach. So we'll have to sleuth at the weekends. But not Sunday afternoons because I'm at Heidi's mum and dad's place. With Keith coming out of his moody fog and being a part of the family, I don't want to miss the family Sunday roast."

"You work every evening?"

"Four weeks of five evenings a week. Mr Morris says that I am the most logical as I'm single. Didn't I tell you this?"

He ignored her question, honing in on the other bit. "But you're not single."

"I meant the non-married teachers," she said airily, waving her hand.

"Hmm, well, that only leaves Saturday. I'm sure you'll want to spend it with whatever his name is."

"Probably," she agreed with zero conviction.

"Look, Friday evening class finishes early, at six. There will be a couple of hours before it gets dark to wade around Turner land to work out who these two are."

"All right, but that means we won't see very much of each other."

"That's what being grown up is like, Luke."
"Sucks."
"It does."

5

Freya

Two weeks had passed since she stood in front of two blank headstones. Freya had been avoiding Luke because she didn't have a good enough reason for her fake fiancé to still be away.

Freya stood at the bottom of her staircase, used one hand to hold on to the bannister and let it take the weight as she flexed her knee to slip on her black-heeled shoes. One after the other, she pushed them on. Standing tall, she took a couple of steps to the long oval mirror and swiped on lip gloss.

It was Thursday, and her evening class beckoned. She couldn't wait to have all of her evenings back. Not that there was a lot to do now her best mate was loved up at the mansion. But still, teaching kids and the odd adult life skills and French wasn't the best way to spend two hours after a full day of teaching.

Freya put on a short leather jacket with no adornments,

not even a zip, her handbag over her shoulder, and she was ready to go. One final look at her hair, and she caught the twinkle of the ring on her finger. For a heavy ring, it never moved even a little bit on her finger. Freya loved it and would keep up the ruse as long as possible because she had beauty on her finger.

Swiping her keys off her hook by the door, she was on her way to the school. With pencil-thin heels, she opted for the road instead of the pavement. Nothing, if she could help it, would ruin her navy suede heels. She hadn't changed out of her navy pencil skirt but had swapped her cream blouse for a navy fitted t-shirt. The jacket was cream suede.

Freya loved beautiful things. She worked hard to have a wardrobe filled with clothes she loved. She paid a fortune for shipping, but what else would she spend her money on?

Football practice was happening in the gym, so the school was already open when she arrived. The old building was rock solid and freezing cold every day of the year. But it had a charm she loved. As a pupil at the school, she often wore layers under her school uniform with thick tights. While others sat in class wishing, they could put their coats on. Wearing coats in class wasn't allowed back then and wasn't allowed now. So when she had to take hers off, she was still toasty.

Now she could hug a thermal mug with its own mat to keep the contents warm and her hands. She wasn't going to show weakness in front of these kids.

Shouldering the classroom door, she shoved it open and kept her foot at the base to wheel the case in and hold on to her coffee mug.

"All right, settle down. Try to behave. There are adults coming to class this evening, not just you rowdy lot."

She pulled the case on wheels to the chair sitting behind

her desk and parked it to one side. Five school kids were mucking about at the back, playing a game she didn't understand. They shuffled around, looking like they weren't allowed to engage with the others. Like they were opposite magnets. Another kid sat on his own behind a desk and looked bored out of his mind.

She knew why all six were there. It was a mass fight in the hallway a week ago. As punishment, they were assigned five evenings of life lessons and French.

Very few adults signed up for evening classes at the school, so she inflicted her life skills on the kids who were in detention. The schoolchildren went home first, ate their dinners and then came back. During the winter, she had a full turn-up as there wasn't much else to do, but as soon as the weather changed, she had a litter of excuses fall onto her desk.

She was three kids down but had three adults attending.

"Miss, why have we got the oldies coming?"

"They're not old," Freya replied. "They're my age."

"Exactly," the kid mumbled.

"Hey, make yourself useful and push the tables and chairs to one side of the room. The side that doesn't have the plug sockets."

That side was the window. Groans and complaining echoed around the room as sulky teenagers dragged the tables instead of lifting them, making screeching and scraping noises for a solid two minutes. By the time they were done, she had a headache forming.

The door opened, and three adults walked in. Two retired men had recently lost their wives and were learning how to fend for themselves.

And Luke Turner.

"What the hell are you doing here?" she demanded.

He looked freshly showered, his hair a little damp. Dressed in dark jeans and a white shirt open at the neck. It was one of those shirts with no collar. He wore it loose over his jeans. Then she gazed at his boots that were kicking the floor. It was his innocent smile that had her eyebrows knitting.

A chorus of heckles came from the kids.

"Hush, you lot," she barked out.

Then a chorus of laughter.

"Is that how you greet all your students?" Luke asked, sauntering in like he'd attended all her classes.

Freya walked towards Luke while the other two men joined the school kids who had hefted up onto the tables shoved to the side. She had a peanut gallery.

"Not usually, but you're you. Why are you here?"

"You have ignored me for two weeks. I've assumed you have been spending time with your fiancé, but I've missed you. If this is the only place I can spend time with you, then so be it."

"You can't be here," Freya insisted.

"Why not? I've paid my money. I can be here. The kids are here. Those two men are here. I can be here. I'm ready to learn life skills."

"Oh man, you are too much," Freya muttered. "Come with me. We need to grab the ironing boards."

"What?"

"Tonight, we learn to iron shirts and some other things."

"What other things?" he asked as he followed after her out of the room.

"Kids, behave while I'm gone. I'll be able to hear you, so keep things civil," Freya shouted over her shoulder. When she looked back, she was startled to see Luke very close.

"I'll keep a watch on them," Bobby, one of the older gentlemen, said, tapping his nose.

Five of the kids aimed their groans his way but didn't move from the desks. The sixth kid, Kenny, dropped his shoulders. Freya didn't miss that.

"Come on, trouble," she said to Luke and strode down the hallway.

The supply cupboard wasn't far. When she got there, it was unlocked. A silent thanks to the premises staff for getting her note.

Freya walked into the dark room, pulled the drawstring above her and tilted her head to see where the ironing boards were kept. She tiptoed towards them when she spotted them and then kicked the bottom.

"What are you doing?" Luke asked, his shoulder leaning against the doorframe.

He had his arms crossed, and his hip cocked, one side dropping down.

"Telling the spiders I'm here. Giving them a chance to run for it."

"Still scared of the beasties?"

"That's your fault, Luke. You locked me in the vault and wouldn't let me out. All those webs told me there were spiders bigger than my head."

"The door jammed. You were in there for thirty seconds, max."

"Enough time for all the creepy crawlies to run over me. I still swear a tarantula dropped on my head."

"There are no tarantulas on Copper Island."

Not satisfied, she kicked the ironing board again.

"So you say."

"So the scientists say."

Freya huffed and lifted the first ironing board, and brought it over to Luke.

"Hold that," she said with a sour face.

"You're cute when you're angry, not letting go of something that happened when we were eight."

"I have a long memory."

She brought over three more boards and clapped her hands together to get rid of the dust.

"Let's go. You can carry them as punishment."

"What for?"

"All the scrapes you got us into over the years."

"You liked those times. I miss those times. Speaking of which, when will we work on the gravestones?"

"What about Saturday? I have the day free, and it looks like it will be good weather."

"It's a date."

Luek took two boards under each arm and marched them back to the classroom with Freya following. She took more notice than usual at his powerful arms carrying the boards like they were made of cardboard.

They entered the room to find all eight of the occupants in silence, swinging their legs back and forth.

"I miscounted. I need another one. Can you get these set up? The irons are in the case by my desk."

"Sure. Do I get a reward for helping?" he asked.

Freya looked around the room to see a row of amused faces.

"What reward do you want? I might consider it."

"Is your fiancé working here tonight?"

"Why would he be working tonight?" she asked.

"He's a teacher, right?" Luke said evenly.

Shit. She'd forgotten that lie.

"There are no single male teachers in the school, Mr Turner," one of the kids helpfully offered.

Freya made a mental note to give the kid detention every time he broke any rule. No leniency for him. She swung her gaze over the kid and back to Luke.

"I never said he was a teacher," Freya said.

It made things ten times worse because Luke's grin widened so much that he was devilish. Freya usually backed away when he broke out that grin, but today she had the delinquent kids looking at her, waiting for a reply.

"Plug your irons in and ensure they sit on their ends. I don't want us burning down the school. Cynthia Turner would not be impressed that her family's donation was in ashes because we couldn't iron a shirt," she ordered.

Freya wimped out and got back to work.

Luke's grin was now approving as he nodded.

"Find your pairs."

Freya watched as Luke looked around the room at his options. He strode over to the quietest kid in the room. Kenny. He muttered something to the boy. Round eyes and an open mouth responded to whatever Luke had said. The older gentlemen paired up, and so did the other kids, making a two and a three team. There was minimal shoving. Instead, the five boys, thick as thieves on a bad day, looked over at Luke and Kenny. They weren't so smug now.

If Luke paired with Kenny, the other five made two teams, and the older gentlemen made a pairing, she wouldn't need another ironing board.

Once they were all set up at their stations, Freya opened her other suitcase and draped four white shirts over her arm. She circled the room to each pairing and gave them their shirts. Luke and Kenny were last in the semi-circle.

"Are you okay with being paired with Luke Turner?" she asked Kenny.

"Yes, Miss Riley," he replied immediately.

"Do you know this man?" she asked.

Freya knew Luke hadn't been back long, but maybe Kenny had been with his dad up at the estate and met Luke then.

"We've met before, Miss," he said.

"Oh?"

She directed her question to Luke.

"We met the morning I got off the boat. It's a small island. I'm bound to meet everyone eventually, Miss Riley," Luke said.

There was that grin again, making her flush. She wished he'd turn it off in public.

What he said was true, Freya reasoned. Still...

"All right. Get ironing, and while you're producing the perfectly ironed shirt with no tram lines, we'll go through what we learned on Tuesday. I want the American states."

Luke rubber-necked around the room, looking for answers to what Freya was talking about. Kenny muttered to Luke, and he nodded.

"We'll start with Luke and Kenny."

"Virginia," Kenny said.

"North Carolina," Luke said.

And so it carried on while they ironed they took turns to recite the American states. Then it was South American countries. Finally, they moved on to European capital cities. By the time their memories had run dry, the shirts were done. They weren't perfect, but a good effort was made. Freya went around the room to inspect their efforts and openly laughed at Luke's effort.

"You'd wear a jacket, right, if that was something you'd wear?" Freya said.

"No, I'd get Maggie to do it," Luke replied like she'd asked an absurd question.

"When you get yourself a wife, she will not iron your shirts and won't allow Maggie to do it. So I'd suggest you have another go."

"How certain are that my wife won't iron my shirts," Luke asked, head tilted, eyes sparkly with a mischievous grin.

Freya was silenced. She didn't know where her certainty came from and had no answer. That was another lie. She'd answered like she would be his wife, and she had no plans to do his ironing.

Ignoring his question, she continued her instructions.

"Okay, let's get these irons unplugged and put to the side. Fold the boards and rest them against the wall at the front. Then get the tables and chairs back to their proper places."

Luke cackled from the back while he reached over to the plug socket. She gave him a glare, but he didn't see her. But the other kids did and laughed behind their hands.

"I think I'm enjoying detention," one of the gang said.

Luke's head turned when he straightened and looked at the kid who spoke.

"This is detention?" he asked, raising his eyebrows.

"Yeah, Miss makes us learn life stuff while we have detention. The other teachers make us do our homework."

"How many other teachers are there who cover detention?" Luke asked.

Freya wanted to blurt out it was a trick question but kept her mouth shut.

"Seven. They're on rotation," the delinquent kid volunteered.

"And you've been in them all?"

"Yeah," he mumbled.

"Don't you ever learn to stay out of trouble?"

"I think the island's definition of trouble is not the same as the rest of the world."

"What did you do this time?"

The kid didn't answer and shifted his gaze to Kenny. Luke followed the trajectory, his eyes narrowing, his face turning annoyed.

"Again?" he said, raising his voice. "After we last spoke?"

"He started it," the kid protested.

"I bet there was a reason why," Luke clipped out. "Do we need to have another chat?"

"No, Mr Turner," the kid replied.

"You sure about that?"

"Certain."

Luke kept his gaze on the kid and then swept through the last of them and finally to Kenny.

"Did you really start it this time?"

Kenny nodded.

"Good for you," Luke replied.

Freya was about to protest when Luke's eyes swung her way. They were intense, so she kept quiet. She'd never seen Luke that intense before, not even after a session with his aunt.

The other adults moved the boards to the front. The delinquent kids moved the tables and chairs while Luke spoke quietly with Kenny. It was all Luke talking while Kenny listened, nodded in places, and finally dropped his head and sighed.

"We clear?" Luke said in a louder voice.

"Yeah, Mr Turner," Kenny said, and oddly, his face brightened.

Freya was desperate to know what had gone down. She'd never seen Kenny look so optimistic or look at the other kids without fear in his eyes.

Whatever Luke did was a marvel.

Later when the class was over, Luke helped her to take the ironing boards back to the cupboard, put the irons back in the suitcase and shove the shirts as tightly as possible in a pillowcase, ready for the next outing of how to iron a shirt. It turned out they were all a lot better at ironing a shirt than balancing their bank accounts. Each of them had a fake bank statement and a pile of receipts. None of them balanced. The whole class was laughing at Freya's exasperation.

They were walking back to her classroom, where he took the suitcase on wheels from her hand while she locked up her classroom and kept it in his hand while they exited the school and strolled down the quiet road to her place.

"I really enjoyed the class. You looked good at the front, keeping their minds active while they got through two hours of punishment."

"They're good kids, really, just bored. I'd like a week where one of those five kids isn't in one fight or another. Or skipping school or giving the staff backchat. The list is endless. Far worse in the winter. I swear they deliberately act up, so they have somewhere warm to go in the evenings. Those kids don't have the best home life."

"That's a shame. They need a hobby or a job that keeps them active."

"Not a lot to do on the island during the off-season. I'm sure they'll be on the first boat off here when they finish their education."

"I don't doubt that."

"What did you say to Kenny?"

"Guy talk, you wouldn't understand."

"Please don't tell me you're going to teach him how to fight?"

Luke gave her an expression of hurt, even stopping in the middle of the road to put his palm flat on his chest.

"I would never..." he said like she'd wounded his pride.

"Oh god, you are. I don't want to know. Leave me out of it."

"I'm not going to show him how to throw a punch. He's fourteen. I have an idea, though. I need to talk to the others first. If they agree, I'll talk to you next to see if it interferes with their schooling, rules, and shit."

"Wow," Freya said.

"What?"

"You're following rules?"

"Yeah, kind of have to on an oil rig, boring as fuck, but it weened me off constantly wanting to break all the rules."

"Ah, you see kindred spirits in those kids."

"Maybe. But they don't seem to have a dad or a mum steering them on the straight and narrow. They are each other's best friends, so there is no voice of reason. I had a great dad and the best of best friends, and I don't think they have that."

Freya stopped in front of her house and looked at Luke standing in the middle of the road. He was looking around like he hadn't said the sweetest thing. They didn't do emotional talk. Ever. It was boisterous, tree climbing and getting into trouble with his aunt. Writing letters about what was happening in their lives. Not once did Luke tell her she was the best of best friends. His brothers and sister were the shit. Pride burst in her chest at the words.

"Luke," she said.

"What?"

This was said in a normal tone like she was about to ask him if he wanted an apple or an orange.

"Nothing. You coming in for a coffee?"

"Sure. You have any biscuits?"

"Absolutely."

Luke gave her a beaming smile and wheeled her case up to her front door, and lugged it inside once she'd got the door opened.

6

Luke

"You're filthy," Luke said, watching Freya on her hands and knees, feeling the grass over the two plots in front of the unmarked grave stones.

He couldn't take his eyes off her swaying hips as she moved. Did she always move so gracefully? He couldn't say he had ever noticed. That damn ring on her finger glinting in the sunlight reminded him he shouldn't be thinking of her that way, even if he was sure she had made the man up.

If she had made him up, she had something to hide.

But his aunt was sure hiding something bigger if his siblings didn't know about these graves. Aunt Cynthia absolutely knew.

But he was fucked if he was going to ask her.

"I've got my least favourite clothes on. It doesn't matter. I want to see if there are any clues below the grass line, maybe initials."

"I'm guessing whoever wanted these here knows who is

in the ground. What I don't understand is why there are two. Surely they'd use the same plot?"

"Maybe they died a while ago, and there is no one down there, and these are symbolic."

"With no words?"

"I did a little research. There have been deliberately unmarked graves over the centuries. Some because the family didn't have much money, they could only afford the headstone. Clearly, that's not the case with your family, as your family is the richest family in the land, not counting the King."

"Quite."

What else could he say? He couldn't deny he came from a rich family, not that he saw any cash from it. But he never took for granted a full stomach, clothes on his back and a roof above his head until he could get the fuck off the island and earn his way.

"In Ireland, there is a gravesite that has big rocks to show who is buried where. The families know the boulder that looks like a loaf of bread is Uncle Bertie, who spent all his time up in the hills tending his sheep."

Luke chuckled as Freya sat back on her calves, swiped her hand free of the dirt and placed her hands on her hips.

"Nothing," Freya said.

She curled her feet under her, moved into a crouch and then stood in such a smooth move he wanted to applaud. He was stunned at her agility, and she didn't do any yoga classes he knew about.

"What?" she asked.

Snapping out of his daze of Freya in tight workout gear, he glanced back to the gravestones, and an idea popped into his head.

"We need to find Copper Island's gravedigger. Someone

had to dig the graves, and it wasn't my aunt. Likely wasn't Bailey either at his age."

"I don't know who digs the graves at All Saints Church or your chapel. Reverend Sprite might know," Freya suggested.

"That's a good idea. Let's go see if she's in."

"I need feeding first, Luke Turner. We should pop by and see Maggie," Freya suggested.

"Maybe another time. Let's see if Jason's in Edward Hall kitchens. He can make us breakfast."

"Oh, good idea," Freya said, her eyes lighting up.

Luke knew why she was instantly interested and was happy he could disappoint her. The elite endurance guys had checked out, vowing to come back again.

He wouldn't let Freya know until she asked him where they were. He had to have some fun.

There was no fiancé. He was absolutely sure.

He took her hand and instantly dropped it and then strode ahead of her to cover his automatic contact without seeing her reaction. Luke didn't know what was going on in his head and wanted to go back to when he was home when it was normal between them. He'd give her a piggyback, and she would throw an arm around his neck and kiss his head.

"Hey, wait up," Freya called out.

He could hear her flip-flops flapping as she jogged to catch up. They took the long way around, not risking seeing Aunt Cynthia and entered Edward Hall via the front. Crossing the foyer, Freya looked up and around.

"It's very quiet," she said.

"Big place, babe."

"Still, testosterone-fueled men would make some noise."

And there it was, Freya wanted to see the hot guys.

"They've been gone for a few days," Luke replied with a

playful grin. "Why do you care, anyway?"

"Well, I don't. It was an observation. When is your next booking?"

She was covering for her disappointment, poorly.

"More hot guys are coming next week. Never fret. The professional gig racers have booked out the place."

Luke glanced at Freya to catch her beaming smile aimed at the floor.

"Will your fiancé be back by then?"

The smile slid off her face, and he could see the cogs whirring in her head at a response.

"He might have come and gone away by then. His work takes him at odd times for unknown periods. Difficult to tell."

"Does he plan on staying in that mysterious job when you're married?"

"Presumably. I'm not the type of woman who dictates what a man should do."

"But you don't want an absent father when you have kids, surely?"

Freya quietened as we entered the deserted kitchens. No Jason, meant no breakfast.

Freya remained quiet when we crossed the floor, pushed out of the emergency exit, and then walked across the lawns to Turner Hall. Freya was leading the way. I didn't want to enter the grand house, but clearly, Freya did.

"Will Maggie have some Weetabix and coffee?" Freya asked quietly.

"Almost certainly," Luke replied, now kicking himself for pushing the subject.

Now he thought the fiancé was real, and he'd hurt her feelings or at least had given her food for thought.

"I imagine it will be difficult with him away so much. If it wasn't for your letters, I would have been constantly worried about you," Freya said.

Luke stopped in the grass a hundred feet from the back door to Turner Hall kitchens. She worried about him? He loved getting her letters too. Often when he was abroad, he'd send postcards or a letter, but she always sent her letters to the rig with a kiss on the seal at the back. He knew she'd kissed it because the imprint of her lips in red lipstick was exactly like her lips. Her lips were equally plump. Her cupid's bow was perfection, and when he got her letters, he looked to the seal first.

"There was nothing to worry about, babe. I was always with someone," he said, trying to worry away the burning in his chest with the heel of his hand.

"Words don't stop the worry, honey," she muttered.

They entered Maggie's kitchen, Freya first, and Luke followed her in. Maggie was at the stove like she lived and slept there. Bailey was at the far end in front of the half-wood, half-glass wall. The glass was split into small square sections that allowed you to see through, but it was mottled, so it was all distorted. He'd know if there was someone on the other side but not necessarily who.

"Hi Maggie, hi Bailey," Freya said. "Can we impose for some breakfast? We've been on a scouting trip, and we're famished. I didn't have time for food before I hoofed it up here to see this one," she said, thumbing over her shoulder.

"Take a seat Freya. It's good to see you after so long. I hope we get to see you more often now that Luke is back," Maggie said.

"Me too. I love coming in here. I love my parents and their home, but something about this kitchen makes me want to stay awhile."

"That's lovely to hear, Freya. You're welcome anytime.

Even if Luke isn't around."

Freya beamed at Maggie, and Maggie swung her eyes to him. She tilted her head and raised her eyes, sporting a terrific smirk. He had no idea what message she was conveying.

"Should I bring those boxes down from storage?" Maggie asked.

It was a loaded question, one that I didn't want Freya asking about. She didn't need to know what was in those boxes.

"Not now. I'll come over in the week and get them."

"As you wish. Take a seat, and I'll make some coffee." Then her eyes turned to Freya. "What do you want to eat?"

"Weetabix will be fine, or muesli."

"Nothing warm, like scrambled eggs and sausage?" Maggie suggested.

"Maggie," Freya said low. "Really?"

"Of course."

"I'll have some of that," Luke said, joining Freya on her side of the table on the bench seat.

"I will too, Maggie, if it's not too much trouble."

"No trouble."

Bailey cleared his throat and stalked forward, coming to the country kitchen table. The tips of his fingers of one hand touching the wood. He bounced them there for a few moments and then spoke.

"Miss Turner would like you to see her."

"Can you tell her I politely decline?" Luke asked, knowing what the answer would be.

Bailey would do whatever Luke said, but there was always a word of caution if it wasn't the best route.

"Yes, Sir, of course."

His fingers bounced a few more beats.

"If you change your mind. Would you let me know, and then I can arrange a meeting?"

And there it was.

"I will, Bailey."

"Very good."

"Bailey," Luke said. "Do you know who digs the graves for the Turner family?"

"I believe it's Gilbert Philbott. He does All Saints too."

"Thanks, Bailey. Is there still only one stone mason in town?"

"Same person. He runs the pottery barn as a business. Not enough business in headstones these days as people prefer cremation."

"Thanks. I'll look him up."

"Planning ahead, Sir?"

Bailey was so polite when he asked probing questions. Luke had too much respect to rebuff his questions.

"I'm getting used to the Turner land as, eventually, we'll inherit it. Ticking boxes about who sets the headstones in the gravesite. I saw a few I liked when we raised a glass to Dad."

"I think the Mistress has the local business for the family. Certainly the recent generations."

"Right. Thanks, Bailey."

Bailey left them to do whatever Bailey did, and Freya kept her body sitting forward, but her head turned to him.

"What's in the boxes?"

He knew she wouldn't let it go. It was shocking she waited so patiently to ask him. If he'd realised, he would've kept Bailey talking longer.

"Old memories," he answered.

It wasn't a lie as such, but he felt embarrassed about what was in the boxes.

7

Freya

Sitting in front of a pottery wheel, Freya regretted agreeing to come to the class with Luke. He barely touched her with his bizarre promise not to touch another man's woman.

It only annoyed her because there was no man, and until Luke stopped his tactile habits, she didn't realise how much they hugged, held hands and draped over each other at any opportunity.

Freya looked to her right to see Luke had moulded his piece of clay into something beautiful. A tall, shapely jug that had no handle. He'd even put a dip in the edge for the water to flow out. Freya's was still a lump of distorted mess in the middle of the turntable. Every time she started to peddle, the clay went out of control, and she stopped and watched Luke put the finishing grooves to the middle and top of his creation. Once he was done, he sat back with a pleased grin and wiped his hands on the white apron tied around his waist. Splatters of clay were over his blue t-shirt like a Jackson Pollock painting. It had sprayed along his neck and into his hair.

She was busy taking note of the corded muscles in his forearms when she heard someone clear their throat. Her head snapped up in the direction of the noise. She didn't need to go far, as it was Luke wearing a wicked grin. His eyes were alight with something that caused her cheeks to burn.

Was she caught checking him out?

"What's caught your attention, Peaches?" he asked.

"When did you learn to make pottery?"

"You like it?"

"It's gorgeous, Luke. I think it would make a stunning pitcher or a vase for wildflowers."

She watched as his face lit up at her praise, his eyes warming at her words. Surely he'd been praised before?

"I'm glad you like it. I've never tried pottery before. It's awesome."

"I can't say the same."

Luke looked down at Freya's lump and chuckled.

"Do you want a hand?"

"I don't know what I want to make," Freya confessed, feeling defeated.

"What about a bowl for the pitcher to sit in?"

That was a great idea. She prepared the lump with water and reshaped it into a dome. Luke stood from his place and then dragged his stool to sit behind her. He sat close to her back, so close she could feel the heat from his body on her back. Luke scooted forward so his legs were on the outside of hers, his knees brushing her thighs. Then he rested his chin on her shoulder and rested his hands at her waist.

"Let's go," he said quietly. "Start peddling."

She held back her shiver at his closeness. He'd acted so

extreme to her having a fiancé. Now he was as close as a pillion rider on a motorcycle. Luke's quiet encouragement fanned over her cheek. All she wanted to do was fall back against him and let him take over.

She had to remember she belonged to someone else.

"All right, put your hands on the clay. Get used to the texture."

"What about my ring?"

"It's just a ring. It'll get dirty, and then you'll clean it. Put your hands on the clay."

Freya did as he asked.

"Make a fist with one hand and put the palm of your other on the side of the clay. You're going to push down with your fist, making it a wider and shorter piece of clay."

He was still talking quietly into her ear, resting his chin further over her shoulder, so his chest was now plastered to her back. Her body was rigid to concentrate on the clay in front of her. Gilbert Philbott had already demonstrated how to make the jug and the bowl. The other four people in the class were busy making their creations and paying no attention to Luke as he slipped an arm around her waist, flattening his hand on her belly. His other hand was resting on his leg, just in her peripheral vision.

"That's great. Now slip your thumbs to the centre and push inside, making a well."

"Okay," Freya replied, blowing her stray hairs out of her face but not succeeding.

Luke brought his hands up, smoothed back her hair, and then retied her hair in the ponytail holder as she made a well.

"You're doing so well. Now with one hand inside, use your fingers inside to press against the clay and then the knuckles of your other hand on the outside, and you're going to pull up the sides as well as make it curve out."

"It's going to go horribly wrong, Luke."

"It won't. Just keep focussed. Look, let me show you."

Luke took her one hand and spread her fingers so his were interlaced inside the moving pottery, then he pressed his knuckles next to hers and showed her the action. Finally, when she got the hang of it, he pulled his hands away, placed them on her thighs over her apron, and put his chin back on her shoulder.

"It's looking good. Keep going with that action. Keep the clay at the bottom, so there is a heavy base, and then sculpt the sides, so they come out wide."

"Are you sure this is your first time?"

"I may have done a bit of pottery before," he confessed.

"Luke," she snapped.

"Don't blame me. You'd know I'd done pottery before if you'd paid attention to the letters I wrote to you. Focus, we don't want it wobbly. You can tell me off for lying later. I'm sure lying isn't something you'd ever do. So it's not like the pot calling the kettle black."

Freya kept quiet, concentrating on her fingers slipping against his. It was evident what Luke was referring to. How long until she had to admit there was no fiancé. She shifted on her stool. Luke must have thought she was trying to wriggle away because he pressed closer.

"Keeping fucking still," he whispered in her ear. "You're making me lose concentration."

Freya's concentration had flown out the window with Luke wrapped around her, doing all kinds of new things to her body. It looked like she was doing all the work to make the clay into a wide shallow dish, but she was along for the ride.

"You two make a great team. The pot looks fantastic," Gilbert said as he passed.

"Thanks," they both said.

"I contributed nothing to this enterprise, Luke."

"Then you can pull your weight and charm Gilbert into telling us when he made the headstones and why he didn't carve any names onto them."

"Fine," Freya said with a beaming smile.

Gilbert had turned their way again and frowned. Had he heard what Luke had asked Freya? She ignored the worry inching up her spine and dropped her head back to focus on the bowl. Luke lifted his hands, taking hers with him and sat up straight. One of his hands went back to her belly and rested there, keeping her in place. Did he think she was going to run off? The other rested on his leg, the clay already drying in patches on the back of his hand. Freya felt lost in what she could do. Now that she was aware of Luke rather than him simply existing, she was self-conscious about where to put her hands, body and mind.

"I'll clean up here. You go do your thing with Mr Philbott," Luke said.

Luke didn't move a muscle, his palm flat against her stomach. He squeezed once and then stood, leaving her sitting. She felt the draught on her back as Luke moved away. Freya couldn't explain her instant sadness that he was no longer cocooning her.

There was no time for her to dilly dally about Luke running hot and cold. She had a mission to complete. Freya walked over to where Mr Philbott was stacking utensils into a plastic bowl that looked set to go for washing. Then, straightening her apron without knowing what she would ask, she cleared her throat.

"Hi, Mr Philbott. I wonder if I can ask you a few questions?"

"Sure, Freya. What do you want to know?"

"Have you always made the headstones for the Turner family?"

"I've done a few, thankfully not many."

"How many in total, would you say?"

"Now let's see," he said, tapping his finger from one hand onto his other hand.

He was muttering too low for her to hear the words he was saying. Finally, after a solid minute of counting and recounting, he looked up and made his declaration.

"Four."

Freya wanted to burst out laughing. The man was in his seventies but sharp as a tack. Why it took him two minutes to come up with four was beyond her.

"I'm doing a project about his ancestors for Luke and his siblings. As a few families who served them attached to the Turner family for generations, I'd like to thread in their stories too. Can you tell me which of Luke's family you made headstones for?"

"His dad. A sad time that was, I can tell you. Didn't think I'd be making his father's headstone in my lifetime. I thought my son would have that privilege. I did Luke's grandfather and grandmother and Luke's great-grandfather."

"And are you the only business that makes and erects the headstones?"

"Yes, love. Miss Turner only uses our business as she knows we keep all the information confidential."

Freya wondered if he was giving her a clue.

"One last question, and then I'll let you get on with what

you were doing. Which headstone did your father work on last?"

"I'm not sure, as I'd have to check the records. His memory is not what it used to be. He's ninety-one now. He started as a stonemason as soon as he could at fourteen, which means he would have been working from 1946. Too late for Emma Turner. I know he worked on something for Miss Turner, but I can't think who. I can check and come back to you."

"That would be super helpful. Thank you, Mr Philbott. I'll let you get on. I loved today's lesson. I think I'm going to need a lot of practice. Luke helped me with most of it."

"Ah, you two are a good pairing, always have been."

Mr Philbott patted her arm and turned to work on the rest of the utensils. Strolling away, Gilbert Philbott had given her much to think about. There were no straight answers and more questions than before she started talking with him. Moving back to where Luke was packing up, she watched as he admired the bowl they'd made. He placed the jug he'd made over the bowl without touching it. He nodded and placed it back on the pedestal.

"Did you get any answers?" Luke asked when he noticed her standing and gazing.

"Kind of. We might need a debrief over a pint."

"All right, sounds good. Let me have a quick word with Mr Philbott."

"I'll meet you outside."

Luke nodded and left her to speak with Gilbert. She shouldered her handbag, left the classroom and walked down the corridor of the small barn that housed the pottery classes. She headed for the golf buggy and hopped in to wait for Luke.

A few minutes later, they were on the move, Luke

driving even though it was her buggy. Luke was not to be driven. Anywhere. It had always been that way. Freya didn't care. She liked to be driven.

He parked up at the alley next to Heidi's old home, which was one door down from hers, and they kept walking past her front door and onto The Anchor.

Luke was quiet.

"Are you okay?" Freya asked.

"Sure. You?"

"Yeah," she said.

She was, and she believed his answer too. They hadn't spent a lot of time together over the last nine years, and she was still getting used to his bossy ways.

8

Luke

"Morning Maggie, how are ya?" Luke said as he entered her domain in the bowels of Turner Hall.

"Hello, Luke. Jason's kitchen closed?"

Maggie chortled at her joke and shimmied from side the side as she scrubbed a pan in the sink.

"He doesn't crisp the bacon to my liking," Luke muttered and sat on the kitchen table bench.

"Coffee in the pot, help yourself. I need to win the battle with the dishes."

"You want some help?" Luke asked, flexing his muscles, twisting from side to side.

Maggie was gazing over her shoulder and laughed. "I missed you, son. It's good to have you back."

His heart clenched at the reference. Luke moved to the coffee machine and the personal stack of mugs Erica had put aside just for them.

He loved the kitchen as a kid. It was his haven when he didn't want to be near his grandfather or aunt. The elders, as he called them, would never lower themselves to come into the bowels of the house and enter the service areas. Nothing ever happened when his father was home from the rigs. As soon as his dad was on the boat across to the mainland, his grandfather, Archibald Turner, liked to use his walking stick as a method of communication. His aunt wasn't any better, singling him out for her sniping and swiping. Luke would run to the kitchens when they were on the warpath and cling to Maggie's legs. When he grew older, he wrapped his arms around her waist and hid his face against her chest. She never, not once, turned him away. She always hugged him back and let him stay in her kitchens for as long as he needed to. When he calmed enough, Bailey would escort him to his bedroom to ensure he got there safely from the physical and verbal tirade his grandfather and aunt piled on him.

He hated Cynthia and Archibald. Hated that they thought it was okay to bully him. He never saw them do it to Archer or Jason. Luke begged Daisy to tell him if she ever suffered at their hands, but she always denied any harm.

Whenever they could, they stuck close, but the age gap prevented this with school years when his older brothers were in secondary school, and he was still in junior school.

Getting off the island was his priority, like it was for his siblings, but he never wanted to come back. Thankfully he only had to tolerate his aunt, and she was in hiding.

"All right, Luke, in what form do you want your bacon?" Maggie asked when she'd finished scrubbing.

"In a bap with brown sauce. If you have any hash browns, I'll love you forever," he said.

"I have all of those things. Take it easy, and I'll start

cooking. Do you want me to bring down the boxes for you to look through?"

"Um, no, not yet. Can you hang onto them for a while longer?"

"This is a big house, Luke, but my rooms are small. So I keep tripping over them. If I break my leg, how will you get your bacon?"

"Such a gloom merchant, Maggie. I've seen your rooms, they're palatial. I promise to take them soon. I haven't unpacked yet from the stuff arriving from the other house."

"Is it sold?"

"Yeah, we completed a week ago. Feels odd, knowing this is our only home."

He had imaginary straps snap onto his wrists. Again, the feeling of entrapment coursed through him. Luke shivered, mentally shaking off the shackles.

"You can always buy somewhere on the mainland."

"Not likely. The proceeds of the house have been split four ways. I have savings from the rigs but not enough to buy something decent. Anyway, my job is here, and so is my family. I'm not looking to move away."

"That is great to hear, Luke. Now, here is your breakfast. I need to get into town. Do you need anything else?"

"Did I keep you by demanding food?"

"No, Son, don't be silly. I have hours to get to the butcher, and I have a buggy, so it takes no time at all now."

"She's a menace in that thing. We should instal seatbelts," Bailey said, coming into the kitchen and scowling at Maggie.

"They have fitted seatbelts. Keith put them in all the buggies," Maggie said.

Luke chuckled behind his hand as he saw Maggie roll her eyes. He loved these two people. Chalk and cheese, but they would never want to work anywhere else, with anyone else.

"I'm going to head off as soon as I've eaten this," Luke said.

"Can I have a word when you've finished?" Bailey asked.

Luke knew what this was about, so he nodded and ate his sandwich slowly to put off Bailey being fatherly and urging him to do the right thing. Maggie gave a pointed glare to the back of Bailey's head while tugging off her apron.

She knew too.

Maggie left the kitchen tossing her bunch of keys, and Bailey busied himself making a cup of tea.

He settled opposite Luke, waiting patiently for him to finish.

"What did you want to speak to me about?" Luke said after his final mouthful.

"Miss Turner wishes to speak to you."

"No."

Bailey exhaled through his nose and looked down at his cup.

"She's not the same woman, Luke."

"She is exactly the same woman, Bailey. I know she's your employer, and you can't say anything negative because it would go against your standards. However, she is still the same woman from when I was a child and teenager."

"That was a long time ago."

"Not really, Bailey. I'm thirty-one. I've been away a long time, but I swear to you, being in the same room as her makes me feel like those twelve years never happened."

"I'm sorry," Bailey whispered to his cup.

"You didn't hand out beatings, Bailey. There was nothing

you could do. I don't blame you. I was grateful for you and Maggie hiding me away when I needed to disappear."

"I can't not ask, Luke," Bailey said quietly.

"I know that. And because you saved me a hundred times over when Dad was away, I'll meet her."

Bailey's head snapped up. "Are you sure?"

"I'll do it for you. Cynthia can't beat me now, she's too old, and I'm too strong."

"Thank you."

"Hide her cane when I have the meeting, will you?"

"Absolutely."

Luke was thirty-one years old and still looked to the door to see if Maggie was already coming back because all he wanted to do was bawl in her arms. Just the thought of meeting Cynthia scared the shit out of him.

"I'll let you know when it's set up," Bailey said, then drained his cup and stood.

Luke stood too, on his side of the table, picking up his empty plate to take to the sink. "The sooner, the better, Bailey."

"Leave the plate, Luke. I'll wash it up."

Luke did as he asked, only because Bailey needed to take care of him.

9

Freya

Freya's classes were over for another school day, and she needed to get away straight after the bell to get to the lavender farm on the other side of the island. Except there was one student who was dragging his heels leaving the classroom.

"Kenny? Everything okay?" she asked.

"Yes, Miss," he replied with so much gloom it squeezed Freya's heart.

His dad, Ralph, worked long hours at Turner Hall. Ralph's mum had left the island after their divorce. Ralph's ex-wife came back to Copper Island periodically, but other than that time, it was just Ralph and his dad.

"You don't sound like everything is okay."

"Is Mr Turner coming back to evening class again?"

"I'm not sure, Kenny. Is there something you want to talk with him about?"

Kenny didn't answer, looking at the walls and studying

the periodic table like it was the most fascinating thing in the world.

"Well, if you see him, tell him I still have that problem," he said.

Freya was left open-mouthed as he grabbed his bag from the table and ran through the gap in the tables like a pinball. He flew through the open door. When she couldn't hear the thunder of his feet on the linoleum floor, she pulled out her mobile from her pocket in her dress.

Freya: I need to talk to you.
Luke: Now?
Freya: Do you have time?

The phone rang in her hand, making her jump. She hit answer and lifted it to her ear.

"What's up, Peaches?"

"How well do you know Ralph's son, Kenny?"

"I've met him a couple of times. The first time was when I got off the boat and came home for good and the second time was while adding tram lines to the shirts you made me iron."

She chuckled at his correct assessment of his ironing efforts. Pottery he could make, iron a shirt he could not. But it was the, back for good, that stole the breath in her lungs for a moment. He'd never called Copper Island, home, not ever.

"I have a message for you. Kenny says he still has that problem. What's he talking about?"

"Those little shitheads that were there in the ironing class. I caught them shoving him about when I strolled through High Street. Can't stand anyone being picked on, so I had a chat with them. Didn't see any of them until that class."

"Did you know he's Ralph's son?"

"Yeah. Where is he now?"

"I don't know. Should I be worried?"

"How did he look?"

"He looked miserable."

"Anything physical, bruises, problems moving about?"

"Nope. He shot out of my classroom like his arse was on fire."

"All right. Maybe I'll come and see Miss Riley after school tomorrow. See if she'll let me carry her bag home."

"Luke," she said and chuckled. "You don't have to do that."

"It will be the perfect cover. We're friends. Your fiancé is away, so I'm making sure you get home safely."

"There is no crime on Copper Island, Luke."

"Doesn't matter. This is about Kenny."

"True. Look, I've got to get a move on. I need to get to Lavender Farm to pick up my lavender pots."

"How are you getting there? That's on the other side of the island."

"I have exclusive use of the buggy I used to share with Heidi."

"I'll meet you there. Help you get the pots into your house."

"That's not necessary. I'll be fine."

"I'll meet you there, Peaches."

Freya brought the phone away from her ear to check they were connected. They were not.

"So bossy," she muttered as she slid the phone back into the pocket of her dress.

She looked around the classroom. Tidied away a couple of stray textbooks. She closed and locked her desk drawer and then swiped up her slouchy handbag. Before she left her classroom, Freya picked up her jacket, slipped her arms in and shrugged it on.

If she didn't have a giant rock on her finger, the lining wouldn't have caught, but when her hand came free, she smiled at the sparkle the diamond gave her as she gazed at it. Then she sighed because it was all fake, and she wasn't engaged. She couldn't even muster up a fake fiancé.

Halfway to Lavendar Farm, the buggy bumped over the last slope, and she skidded to a stop inches from Luke. She was not paying attention to what was in front of her, but more to her left, looking out over the cliff and across the water. She turned at the last second to see him.

"Bloody hell, Luke, I could have run you over. What the hell are you doing in the middle of the dirt path?"

He was grinning, standing feet apart with his hands in his pockets. It wasn't often she saw Luke in proper trousers. He looked smoking hot with his buttoned-up shirt and tie loosened at the collar. He'd rolled up his sleeves and looked like he'd done it quickly because there was nothing neat about it. A long dark smear was up his right forearm.

"You are a menace in that vehicle," Luke said.

"Hardly. It won't go more than twenty miles an hour."

"You can still do damage. Move over and let me drive."

"Where's your ride?"

"It went sailing over the cliff about five minutes ago."

"It did not," she shouted, looking left and right.

Luke burst out laughing.

"You're right, it didn't, but it has broken down half a mile away. I took a look, but I really don't know why it stopped."

"You put petrol in, right?"

He gave her a surprised glance. "I'm supposed to fill it with petrol?"

"Luke," she snapped, not knowing if he was teasing.

"Well, fuck," he said, raking his fingers through his hair, his head turning in the direction of the sea. "Maybe it just ran out of fuel."

His head whipped back to her, and he winked.

That wink warmed her insides. He'd never winked at her before. She'd never seen him wink at anyone else.

It was sexy. Very sexy.

"Get in. I'll give you a ride."

Then she got a face-splitting grin.

Was he flirting with a knowing grin?

"I'm driving," he said, trying to shove her over with his hip.

"My vehicle, my rules. I'm driving. Get in, or you can walk."

"If I walk, I'm walking back to Sabrina Lodge."

"I never asked you to come," she replied.

"Come on, Peaches, let's get going. They won't be open for much longer."

He was right, and she was all out of energy arguing pointless conversations after being with the kids all day.

"Fine, but only because kids are exhausting, and you're the biggest kid of them all."

He shone his satisfied grin her way and still shoved her over with his hip. She shuffled along to the other side of the bench seat and folded her arms over her chest. He wrapped an arm around her shoulders and hauled her back to sit flush with him. When he was happy she was close enough, he dropped his arm to rest on the back of the seat and drove one-handed the rest of the way to the lavender farm.

Luke parked up, and they got out of the vehicle. Freya swiped up her handbag and lifted it to put it crossways over her body. Luke fell into step with her and threw his arm around her neck.

"You know you're being super weird, right?" Freya said, looking at the hand she could see to her left and then back to his profile.

"Weird, how?"

"You said you didn't want to touch a woman that belonged to another man."

"That's right, I did say that."

"And here you are with me plastered to your side with your arm around my shoulders."

"That's also correct. But I've always done that. I reckon whoever this guy is, he needs to get used to the fact I've known you forever. We have an unbreakable bond, including hugging, head kisses and arms around each other. Not to mention the occasional piggyback when you're drunk. Although he can carry your arse home if you get drunk."

That was the sweetest thing he'd ever said. She'd felt everything he'd said, but she had never heard it from him. She'd hoped they'd had an unbreakable bond. He didn't talk much about anything, especially in the last seven years since his dad had died right in front of him. Freya wasn't sure what she was expecting. She knew men were different from women. She would've cried and talked Heidi's head off if it had been her that watched her dad die, but men were different. She'd tried to talk to him, but he was too closed off. She accepted it, trusted that they were still the best of friends and hoped one day he would be okay with talking about that day.

"I don't get drunk these days. Heidi is too loved up to go to the pub. It's all changed now she's besotted with her husband. Not that I begrudge her happiness and her to-die-for cottage."

"You like her cottage?"

"I love her cottage. It's off-the-charts sensational. Archer and Erica's cottage is awesome too. I know the shells are all the same for the cottages. But Erica and Heidi's places are so different you don't realise the layout is the same. To die for, honestly, Luke."

She gazed up at him smiling, and he had lost all his humour.

"What's wrong?"

"Nothing. I never knew you liked the cottages."

"Well, I like Archer's and Jason's. I've never seen yours because you are so ill-mannered you haven't invited me around. When's Daisy coming home? Maybe I can get her to go to Friday night drinks, and then I can check out her cottage and see what it's like."

"But you have hated the Turner houses for as long as I've known you. Which is since we were kids."

"I don't think I've ever said I've hated the Turner houses. They're magnificent. Turner Hall is so grand I'd be too afraid to stay very long for fear of knocking over something expensive or saying the wrong thing to Bailey. Edward Hall is just as grand in its clinical whiteness. I've already told you I'd do just about anything to have a cottage like Archer or Jason's places."

"Wow. I must have convinced myself you'd hate it there. It's why I haven't invited you around for dinner."

"Well, now you know. I'll expect my invitation in the post," Freya said, smiling as she nudged him with her hip.

"We're here," he said, pulling open the greenhouse door and letting her enter before him.

10

Luke

Luke was enjoying his morning coffee, sitting on a borrowed chair he'd hoofed down from Archer's back patio area, drinking from the mug he took from Jason's kitchen.

He needed to get furniture for his cottage, so he didn't have to keep stealing his brothers' stuff and annoying their wives. It was this thought of having his own wife that he spotted Bailey striding across the lawn to his place. Bailey didn't waste any time getting the meeting set up.

He sighed tiredly, dropped his feet he had propped up on the low brick wall and placed his coffee mug on the floor. He hadn't managed to procure a table yet. All the furniture would come when the house was emptied.

"Morning, Bailey," Luke said, moving to the opening in the wall to greet him.

They shook hands.

"Morning, Sir," Bailey replied.

"I'd invite you in for a coffee, but I only stole one mug and one chair."

Bailey gave him a warm smile and a soft chuckle.

"I don't have enough time to sit and put the world to rights, although looking at this view, it is very tempting. I'd forgotten how quiet it is here at the lodges."

"You're welcome any time, Bailey. No formality is needed with any of us over here. Maggie too. I hope you know that."

"I do, and it's really good to know you're all coming back to live here. The Turner property needs it. It's too old and too grand to leave to decay and ruin."

They stayed silent for a minute while they gazed across the lawn that had been recently mowed and at the trees that were short enough that they could see the ocean.

"Has she set a date and time?" Luke said eventually.

He knew Bailey had to get back, but only because he always had a long to-do list with a building the size of Turner Hall. Bailey loved working the Turner estate, and he wouldn't do anything to jeopardise it.

"She has, Sir. This morning at ten o'clock in the morning room."

"I'll be there. Well, I'll be there earlier so I can get Maggie to make me breakfast."

"She is hoping you'll do that. It's her way of giving you strength."

He needed to make sure he dropped in more often to see Maggie. He owed her a lot after his mother left the island.

"I'll swing by at nine for a butty and a natter," Luke promised.

"Right you are. I'll leave you to it."

Bailey didn't wait for a goodbye from Luke and walked away. Luke bent to pick up his coffee, pressed a hip to the wooden post at the end of the wall, and rose to the latticework above the patio area. He held onto his ribs with one arm across his torso and the other hand raised the coffee cup to his mouth. This was done slowly, his way of calming his anxiety whenever his aunt was mentioned. He did not want to see her, but his upbringing and respect for Bailey would get his arse in her morning room to hear what she said.

It was still early, not long after seven. Luke had time for a run, a shower and a stroll to get to Turner Hall. So he did just that.

Arriving at the mouth of the kitchen, he heard Maggie's deep chuckle. When he entered through the open doorway, he saw both his brothers sitting on the bench seat at the kitchen table. He felt his heart constrict at the show of support.

"I was just reminding Maggie of the time we all trooped into her kitchen with muddy feet ten seconds after she'd finished scrubbing the floor until it was gleaming," Jason said, shifting up the bench seat.

"Oh man, you were so angry at us. You chased us around the kitchen with a broom," Luke said.

"And that made the floor even muddier," Archer said, throwing his head back laughing.

"I got my own back, making you lot wash down the floor," Maggie replied.

"You did. Never did I enter this kitchen again with muddy feet," Jason said.

"Fun times," Luke said, plonking myself down on the bench next to Jason.

"What am I making you boys?" Maggie said, putting her cup of tea down.

"Finish your tea, Maggie. We can wait," Archer said.

"It's finished. Give me your orders," she said, upending the cup to show it was empty.

"Bacon sandwich," Luke said.

"Yeah, I'll take one of those," Archer said.

"Me too," Jason replied.

"Well, that was easy," Maggie said and marched off to the walk-in fridge in the small room adjoining the kitchen.

"What are you guys here for?" Luke asked.

"Moral support. We think we know why she's summoned you, so we thought we would be here for you," Archer said.

"He didn't do this for me, I hasten to add, but I think we should stick together," Jason said.

"Lord knows what will happen when Daisy gets the call," Archer said.

"She won't go. No matter how much she loves Maggie and Bailey, she won't go," Luke said.

"I wasn't sure you'd go," Archer said. "You don't have to. Bailey will be fine with it."

"She can't hurt me any more than she already has. I'm sure it'll be fine."

Jason and Archer stared at him for a few moments, and then Archer spoke.

"What did she do to hurt you?"

"It doesn't matter. It was a long time ago. It took a long time for me to understand why Mum left us and the island, but maybe she had the best idea. We left, didn't we?"

"We did, and I am struggling to accept that I did. If I had my time again, I would've come back to spend more time with Dad," Jason said.

"Yeah, me too," Archer said.

Luke felt like he'd been punched in the stomach. His brothers didn't know how much those comments hurt. If he had his time again, he'd try harder to save his dad's life. Move more quickly, get the defibrillator on him faster. But he wouldn't get his time back, and it was a fool who wished it.

"Are you sure you just want bacon? What about some cheesy scrambled egg on the side?" Maggie said, coming back into the kitchen, oblivious to the men's conversation.

"I'll take some scrambled eggs. I've already been for a run, so I've earned it," Luke said.

"I went for a surf with Keith, so pile them on Maggie," Jason said.

"I'll stick with the sandwich, Maggie," Archer said.

Luke looked over to the coffee pot and took Archer and Jason's mugs for a refill. He took out his mug from the cabinet above the coffee machine, poured three mugs and set up the machine to make another pot. Taking them back to the table, he placed them within reach of his brothers. Archer and Jason were looking his way but not saying anything.

"Are you okay?" Archer asked.

"Yeah, I think. I'm feeling a bit lost, but I know I'm where I'm supposed to be," Luke replied.

"Have you met Freya's fiancé yet?" Jason asked.

"There is no fiancé, but I don't have enough evidence yet to force her to admit it."

"But you have a plan, right?" Archer said.

"I do. I will meet her after school every day until she is forced to confess her big fat lie or roll out the man of her dreams that put a ring on her finger."

"Are you jealous?" Archer asked.

"Of a fictitious man? Hell no," Luke said.

"But what if he's real? Are you ready to give up your bestie?" Jason asked.

"Hell no again. If he does exist and doesn't like the look of me, he will have to accept we come as a package deal."

Archer barked out a laugh.

"You would never accept that as a deal if you were her fiancé, and she told you she had a male best friend who hugged her all the time and kissed her head."

"Hell no, but we're not talking about me being the fiancé. I'm the best friend."

"Hmm, Jason," Jason said into his coffee mug.

"Breakfast is ready," Maggie said, giving Archer a wink and placing his sandwich in front of him.

Next came two plates for Jason and Luke.

"Whatever happens, boys, I hope Freya isn't a stranger in this kitchen. I've got used to Heidi and Erica popping in. It will be nice to have Freya, too," Maggie said.

"I'll let her know, Maggie. Thanks for breakfast," Luke said.

"Eat up before it gets cold."

Once breakfast was eaten, more stories were told, and then it was time to head up to see Aunt Cynthia. Bailey came through to the kitchen with five minutes to go. Luke went to the bathroom to wash his hands and straighten his clothes, paying careful attention to stray crumbs.

Luke came back out and received nods from his brothers and a once-over from Bailey. He nodded, too, and they were good to go.

Luke followed him up the back stairs, across the marble foyer and entered the morning room after him. Once Luke was inside, Bailey closed the door, staying on the other side. Luke wondered if this was how it felt when someone was locked in a cell.

"Luke," Aunt Cynthia said from the other end of the morning room.

She was on the threshold of the morning room and conservatory.

Wearing her uniform of green slacks and a twinset, she looked well-groomed and ready for battle. Luke wasn't there to argue, but she knew he didn't want to be there at all. The one thing on his side was he was an adult now, no longer the child she could bully.

"Aunt Cynthia," he said, not moving.

"I'm not going to spend our meeting yelling at you. Come down this end, please," she clipped out.

He walked thirty feet from the door to where she was standing. Her hands were clasped in front of her. He noticed her sapphire ring, which looked much like an engagement ring but with no wedding band. Had Jonathan given that to her? She had never mentioned a fiancé or a husband in all the time he'd known her. Trying to remember his childhood, he couldn't recall if she'd always worn the ring. Making a mental note to dig out family photographs, he put his ponderings to the back of his head.

"Why am I here?" Luke said.

"Do I need a reason?"

"You never do anything without reason. You usually can't wait to explain all your moves. So let's get this over with."

"Fine. Come into the conservatory. It's time for you to choose."

"Choose what?"

"You need to find a wife."

"You have a selection waiting for me to pick in the conservatory?"

"Don't be smart, Luke Turner."

"I wouldn't put it past you to have already picked my wife for me. That's the Turner way, isn't it?"

His aunt gave him a glare that shrivelled his insides. She didn't say a word as she moved to a large velvet box. She lifted the lid and placed it to the side.

"Time to pick a ring. When you've found the woman who will be a Turner, you are to bring her here to meet me before you propose."

"No."

"What?" she shouted.

"No. I am not picking a ring. My wife will not wear a Turner ring. You may have corralled Archer into picking a ring, but Jason didn't put a Turner ring on Heidi's finger, and I won't either."

"What do you mean? He chose the diamond solitaire. If it's not on Heidi's finger, where the hell is it? It needs to be returned."

All the pieces of the puzzle fell into place. Or more or less into place. The ring on Freya's finger was Jason's rejected ring. He smiled and gave a soft chuckle.

"You'd better take that up with Jason."

"You tell him I want to speak with him."

"Tell him yourself," Luke replied, making a move to leave.

"You were always the disobedient child. I never understood why your father let you onto the rigs."

"What do those two things have in common?"

"If you did as you were told, you wouldn't have let him die."

"How the hell did you come to that conclusion?"

"If you spent more time studying and getting better grades, you would've been a better medic. His death is on your hands."

"Go to hell," Luke roared and strode from the room.

Bailey had the door open and stepped to the side before Luke reached for the door handle.

"Never ask me to meet with her again, Bailey," Luke bit out as he passed the man.

"Yes, Sir," he replied to Luke's back.

Luke, filled with rage, raced down the back stairs and into the kitchen. He came to a skidding halt seeing his brothers and Maggie. They stopped mid-conversation to look at him. He didn't know the first fucking thing to say. His aunt had said what he was already feeling, what he thought, and it hurt like hell.

"What happened?" Archer said, getting up from the bench.

"She wanted me to pick a ring," Luke said.

"What did you pick?" Jason asked.

"I told her no," Luke replied.

"What else did she say?" Archer asked carefully.

"Nothing. I need to get back and change, then get to Edward Hall to make sure Stan and Opaline have everything ready for our new group arriving."

Luke walked past them and headed for the open kitchen door. He heard Jason call out his name, but he ignored him. Luke had to escape before he roared with the pain in his chest. His aunt always knew how to push his buttons, and Luke had never learned how to ignore them. When Luke was living permanently at the Turner estate, he would run to wherever Freya was to get some good in his soul to eradicate the badness from Cynthia. Freya would be teaching right now, and barging into her class for a hug would be inappropriate, but he badly wanted her comfort.

Instead, he jogged to his cottage, headed upstairs, showered for the second time that day and changed into a suit ready for his working day.

Another thing he hated.

The only shining light of the morning was that now he knew for sure Freya was not engaged. She was wearing a Turner ring, and no Turner had proposed.

Yet.

11

Luke

Luke leaned against the wall outside the school on the opposite side of the road. He had his arms crossed with his eyes fixed on the main door. Thankfully everyone knew who he was and his friendship with Freya. Otherwise, he'd be worried someone would question why he was there at all.

The bell rang in the distance, and he pushed himself off the wall to standing, then shoved his hands in his pockets. As the kids piled out of the main entrance, he strolled across the road and pushed through the thong of boys and girls into the main corridor. There was one thing to be said about schools, they emptied fast. A few stragglers were humping on their backpacks. Staff meandered between classrooms, but mainly the hallway was empty.

A kid ran out of the classroom, running hell for leather. It was Ralph's kid, Kenny.

"Why are you running for your life? Those shitty kids giving you a hard time?"

"No, Sir," Kenny said.

"What's your hurry?"

"Need to get to the main house, Dad's working late, and I said I would meet him in his shed. Do my homework there before we went home for dinner. He doesn't like me being in the house on my own."

"Well, if you can wait five minutes, I'll give you a lift. The buggy is one street over, hang out there, and I'll take you up."

Kenny brightened. "That would be awesome."

"All right. Take off. I won't be long. And it's Luke, not Sir."

"Okay," he said and ran off.

That was the second time he had understood Ralph was sacrificing his home life for the Turners. He needed to talk to Archer about it. But, first, he needed to talk to Freya.

Luke walked to her classroom and peered through the small square glass window to see she was sitting with her chin on her hands, looking to the end of her classroom. He strained to see what she was looking at, but no one else was in the room. He turned the handle, and her eyes came to him. They rounded for a second, and then she smiled.

He felt that smile in his gut. Wanted to bask in its light.

"Hey," Luke said, coming into the classroom and shutting the door behind him.

"Hey, yourself. What are you doing here? Another ironing lesson?"

"Absolutely not. I wanted to talk to you."

Freya stood, shimmied down her dark grey fitted dress, and stepped away from her desk. The hand with the ring was tucked under her elbow.

Her dress was doing all kinds of things, but now wasn't the time to concentrate on that. So Luke came forward until he was toe to toe with her. Luke cupped her cheek and grinned. He was done with her being fake engaged. Luke wanted her single.

"You're a liar, Freya Riley," he whispered.

She didn't move from his touch. She stood her ground. The only indication he knew she had cottoned on to the subject was a minute flare of her nostrils.

"I'm not," she whispered back.

"Show me your hand," he said, taking a step back.

Freya gave him a hand that didn't have the engagement ring on it palm up.

"The other one, Freya," he said.

She put that hand palm up in front of him like she was holding two invisible grapefruits. He took the hand with the diamond and turned it over. He dropped his eyes to the ring and then back up to Freya's face.

"You're not engaged, there is no fiancé, and this ring is not yours," he said.

She couldn't answer without perpetuating the lie, and he knew it. So he nudged the diamond to the left and to the right, but it didn't budge.

Freya watched him. "How did you know?"

"Lots of tiny different things. But one thing I do know, you don't keep secrets from me. If you'd fallen in love, you would've shared that with me. It stung for a while that you would keep your happiness from me, but then you were acting weird and checking out the hot guys. Not to mention no one else has seen this mysterious person."

"Fuck," she whispered.

He held the hand with the diamond, dropped it between them, and entwined their fingers. Then he cupped her cheek with his other hand and stepped back into her space. Her fragrance was light and sweet like peaches and seemed to calm him. She'd always smelled like that, so familiar to his senses.

"It won't come off, Luke. You gave me such a scathing look when I told you I was engaged. I was hurt that you wouldn't think it was possible, so I lied. The truth is I tried it on, and it won't come off."

He loved her confession, delighted that he was free to pursue her.

"Do you like it?" he asked.

"Of course, it's gorgeous."

"You know it's a Turner ring, right?"

"Yeah," she whispered.

"Keep it, Peaches."

"I can't," she said, shaking off his grasp and lifting her hand.

He noticed she didn't move away from the hand cupping her cheek. If anything, she leaned into it as she admired the rock on her finger.

"It suits you. It's beautiful, just like you."

She raised her other hand to demonstrate it wouldn't come down her finger. Luke couldn't care less. There was more jewellery in the Turner vault none of the wives would be able to wear it all in a lifetime. Erica would have the most opportunity when she walked the red carpet, but it would stay in velvet cases for the rest of them.

"Luke," she whispered.

"Yeah?" he whispered back.

"I'm sorry I lied."

"That's okay. I'm sorry you thought I was disbelieving someone would love you. Maybe you'll explain tomorrow why you did because the woman I know, even faced with someone who thought she couldn't bag a husband, wouldn't have shied away from telling them. She wouldn't have cared. What I want to know is, why do you care that I was shocked?"

Freya stayed quiet. Luke didn't expect her to answer, so he let the question settle for a few moments.

Then Luke wrapped the hand holding her diamond around her back and pulled her flush with his body. She was trembling. They'd always horsed around when they held each other. Not ever had they held each other this quietly, this closely and fuck if he didn't love it. Freya slowly placed her hands on his chest. The heat branded him like an iron. It felt like his body wanted to know the feel of her hands everywhere.

"I gotta give Kenny a lift up to Turner Hall. Have dinner with me tomorrow, and I'll update you with what I found about the headstones."

"Okay," she said, slowly nodding.

Luke moved to kiss her head like he always did, but this time he saw her eyes close as he moved. She'd never done that before. It was always a quick press of his lips, and then he moved away. This time Luke tightened his hold and heard her whimper, then he dropped his head and kissed her temple, brushing his lips against the soft skin. Luke left his lips there for a few seconds and then moved a step away. It took a few more moments for Freya's eyes to open, and they were locked on his mouth. That sight went straight to his cock.

Luke was hard for his best friend.

"You can start the rumour that your fiancé decided not to come back to the island but said you can keep the ring. It was a whirlwind romance, and he has been summoned home to marry someone else," Luke told her, holding her gaze.

She nodded, and he walked to the door, opened it and left it open before he walked away, down the corridor and out of the school.

He thought of all kinds of horrible things to get his erection to go away by the time he met up with Kenny. As soon as he was twenty feet away, he saw the kids from the ironing class rocking the golf buggy with Kenny in it.

Erection gone, fury arrived.

"What the fuck are you doing?" Luke roared.

The kids froze in their intimidation tactics and turned their upper bodies to look at him. Then two seconds later, they ran away. It was on the tip of his tongue to call them all pussies for running away, but they were kids, and he'd remembered he shouldn't let out the f-bomb. He knew they said worse, but he was the adult.

"You okay, kid?"

"Yeah. I hope the buggy's okay."

"I'm sure it will be fine. It's seen worse. What were they doing this time?"

"They keep calling me rich boy. Telling me, I should hand over all my money. I tell them that my dad works at Turner Hall, not owns it."

"Those lads need a dose of humility and something to distract them. Leave them to me. Let's get you to your dad. We don't want Miss Riley thinking you can't do your homework."

"No, S-Luke," he said.

Luke hauled his arse into the driver's seat and nodded to Kenny to pull the seatbelt across his lap. He dropped his bag between his feet and buckled up. When they arrived at the back of Turner Hall near his dad's shed, he pulled to a stop.

"Kenny," Luke called out as he exited the buggy.

"Yeah?"

"When your dad is working in the evenings, what do you do when you have finished your homework?"

"Read mainly. Bailey lets me into the library."

Luke smiled. Bailey was a good man.

"Well, I might have something more interesting you can do. I'll ask your dad first if it's okay, and then I'll let you know."

Kenny brightened and shifted his bag further up his shoulder.

"Cool," he said and shuffled off down the path to the gardener's shed.

Luke thought he might be able to kill two birds with one stone.

12

Freya

Freya thought she was going to have a heart attack. The palpitations were making her heart pound out of her chest.

"All right, babe, pull down the front of your dress," Heidi said.

Freya did as she was asked.

"Oh, that's a nice bra. Did it come with matching panties?" Heidi asked.

Freya was too panicked to answer and looked at the equipment in the room.

They were in her nurse's room. Freya eyed the bed with stirrups with caution. It was enough to put her off having children. Freya didn't mention anything because Erica was sitting on a chair, stroking her belly, looking at the bed with unadulterated fear.

Heidi lifted the end of the stethoscope and placed it on Freya's chest.

"Bloody hell, warn a girl. That's freezing."

Heidi laughed, brought the circular end to her mouth and, breathed on it, then placed it back on Freya's chest. It was no warmer. Heidi listened as she looked left and right, not directly at Freya. Was this good news or bad news? Then she took it away and, like all doctors, and slung it around her neck.

"Well? Do I need a cardiogram?"

"No, you need a paper bag. You're having a panic attack."

"Is that all?" Erica piped up from her side.

Freya swung to face Erica. "Isn't that bad?"

"Nah, I always had them before I went up for an award or had to walk the red carpet. They have people backstage just for the very purpose of calming us the fuck down. It's not life or death, but the wrong pose and your career can be over."

"Yikes. So tell us, what has your heart all a flutter?" Heidi asked way too innocently.

"Nothing," Freya said quietly, pulling her dress back up her shoulders and turning so Erica could zip her up.

"Come on, you burst into my antenatal appointment and declared you're having a heart attack."

"Sorry, but you did text to say you were done for the day and could gossip."

"True."

"Luke knows there is no fiancé," Freya blurted.

"Oh?" Heidi said, grinning. "How did he find out?"

"Something about me never keeping secrets from him."

"I bet there was something else, but you are a shit liar," Heidi commented.

"I feel… I don't know how I feel."

"About lying?"

"No, not the lying…"

"Freya, what happened?" Erica said.

They scooted closer.

"He got close," Freya said.

"Did he kiss you?" Erica asked, all swoony.

"No, well, no more than the usual head kiss, but it seemed this one was in slow motion, and we were chest to chest with his arm wrapped tight around me."

Heidi put her hand on Freya's knee. She felt grounded, and her heart was slowing.

"You've been in love with him for forever. Why are you freaked?"

"It's been a long time since I've mooned over Luke Turner," Freya said.

"Granted, it might be a few years, but you two are thick as thieves," Heidi said.

"I know, but he has never held me like that before. It felt intimate."

"And he didn't kiss you?" Erica pushed.

"No. Luke wants to meet for dinner tomorrow to go through some papers for our latest puzzle. Some family thing. Did you know he can throw clay and make pottery?" Freya asked Heidi.

"No, is he good?" Heidi asked.

Freya chuckled at her question and then reddened as she associated it with sex.

"Was it like a scene from Ghost?" Erica asked, gushing with hearts in her eyes.

"Oh man, you've been in movies too long. But yes, it was kinda intimate too. Fingers sliding together. Luke was as close as you would be on a motorcycle behind me. I was mesmerised by his skill."

Erica shifted on her seat and said, "Maybe I should get Archer to pottery class."

Freya harrumphed. "Can we focus, ladies?"

"It sounds like he might be into you when you've stopped being into him. Timing sucks. Just tell him you don't like him being this touchy-feely," Heidi said.

"Well, I didn't say that," Freya hedged.

"I knew it. You're hot for him. Just think, if you two get married, we'll be neighbours. We'll all be neighbours raising our families. Our kids will be cousins and grow up together. The cottages will be filled with laughter," Erica said.

Her wistful musings had her staring off into the distance.

"Slow the hell down, hormone lady," Freya said. "He may not be into me."

Erica and Heidi shared a look.

Heidi broke the staring contest and brought her eyes to Freya. "I bet that ring on your finger stays there when you say your vows to Luke Turner. You heard it here first."

Erica nodded, tears dripping down her cheeks, and swung her back to the bed with stirrups.

"How long do these hormones last?" Freya said to Erica.

"Until menopause, apparently, then they turn to rage hormones. Embrace the happy tears while you can."

They all laughed at Erica's over-the-top emotion.

13

Luke

"Did Jason cook this?" Freya said, pointing her fork to the thermos bowl.

"I am wounded," Luke replied.

He'd slaved over the noodle soup, practising several times before he was happy with the taste. It was Jason's handwritten recipe, but Luke had bought the ingredients and made the chicken noodle soup.

"You made this?" she asked with a groan, her eyes half closing.

The sound alone had his dick paying attention, added with the first signs of an orgasm heightening. He was lost, mesmerised by Freya. Seeing her this way was jarring but welcome. If only she knew what she looked like when she was enjoying her food made by his hands.

"Yeah, do you like it?"

"It's sensational."

Luke wanted to punch the air, but he stayed where he was on the bench of the boat he'd taken her out on.

For the evening, he'd borrowed a boat from Keith, Jason's best mate. Collected Freya from school and walked her home carrying her bag. She kept side-eyeing him like he was insane, but he was out to impress her. They'd driven in her buggy out to Keith's shack to get the keys, and now they were slouched out on the benches eating chicken noodle soup.

"It's been so long since I've been out on a boat. I take it for granted that it will always be an option and then never do it," Freya said.

"Now that I'm back, I'll make sure we take a boat out to eat dinner more often until the weather turns in late autumn."

"Yeah, not a fan of choppy water," she said.

Luke sat and watched Freya twist up her noodles with her chopsticks without dropping a single piece of food and eating it. She was so expert he didn't dare try to get liquid down his shirt. He kept it safe and used a fork.

When they were finished, he took her bowl, screwed on the lid and put them in the hamper. Next, he brought out two flasks, two mugs and a plastic box. Then he lifted out a blanket and a folder. Luke was on several missions at once, so he didn't risk looking at Freya in case he got stage fright.

He needed to show her the work he'd done with the online ancestral website. Then he needed to kiss her to see if she kissed him back.

"Come and sit down here. I've got something to show you," Luke said.

He grabbed the blanket and wafted it out, so it lay in one sweeping motion. Freya clapped at his one-sweep motion and then dropped to her knees and then her hip. At any other time, before he saw the ring on her finger, he would've hauled her over to sit next to him, slung an arm around her shoulders and huddled together to look at what he'd found. Now everything was awkward, even if it was only from his side. Everything was amplified.

Spring had arrived super early, which meant lighter clothing on Freya. Which was hell on earth when Luke couldn't touch her the way he wanted to touch her. The skin flashed between her blousy top and her long skirt. Just a sliver of skin, but he wanted to trail his fingers along just to see how soft she was.

"You'll need to get closer so we can look at my tablet screen," he said.

Freya crawling on her hands and needs was almost the death of him. She wasn't looking at him as she prowled to the space beside him. Freya arranged herself with her back to the bench behind them that ran the length of the boat. Luke got brave, wrapped his arm around her waist to pull her to his side, and told her to bend her knees. When she was in position, Luke mirrored her position and rested his tablet on his right leg and her left leg.

"I don't know what to make of what I set up. There are leaves everywhere," Luke said.

Freya moved her head to look at him, and they were inches apart, so close he could lean in and kiss her. Luke needed to save that until later on.

"What did you do?"

"I signed up to an ancestry website. You put your name in, and then parents and so on with what you know, and then they find the rest."

"How far did you get?"

"For now, I put in my parents, grandparents and Aunt Cynthia."

"Anything fruitful come back?"

"Not an awful lot, but you can see who lived at Turner Hall at each census. The latest shows who lived here, in 1921, and then it goes back every ten years. I thought we could map the headstones to the family tree, see who is left, and then dig around for birth and death certificates. They're listed on here but only names. We can apply for them if any sound interesting."

"I cannot wait to do that. Do you remember when we went hunting in the graveyard for the florins?"

"We never did find the treasure. Based on the letters I found in grandfather's study, I still think they were in that cove."

"We could go for another hunt. That cove is massive," Freya said.

"Saturday?"

"Yeah, it's been too long since we fooled around without a care in the world."

They fell into silence as Freya tapped around on the family tree the website populated as each match was found. Finally, she brought the tablet to her lap and snuggled in closer. Luke pulled her closer and kissed her head like he had done hundreds of times over the years. It was so routine Freya didn't acknowledge the touch.

Except for this time, Luke wanted to keep her at his side every night. He idly watched while her tapping increased, inputting names of his family and hitting search. Her breathing was getting shallower as her fingers flew across the screen.

"Luke, Luke, Luke," she chanted.

"I'm right here," he said, chuckling.

"Your aunt ever get married?"

"Christ no, who the hell would marry her?"

"What about children?"

"What?"

"You've got a hint here that says there is a possible match for Cynthia Turner. Look, there's the green leaf. What do you think it means?"

Fury raced through his veins so fast he thought he might have a heart attack. His heart was beating so fast.

"She's got a child?"

"She has something. When I click on it, it won't go anywhere."

"What are you doing tomorrow after school?"

"Marking, but that's about it."

"Right, I'll pick you up from school, and we'll go straight to the graveyard while we have the light. Then I'll cook you dinner while you mark the delinquent's homework. That work for you?"

"Yep, that works. I wanna know what secrets Cynthia is holding," Freya said, gazing at Luke's face like they'd stumbled on a massive clue.

"My guess is we'll either never know, or we'll find out after she's buried."

14

Freya

Luke lifted her bag onto his shoulder and then over his head, so it draped crossways. Freya skipped along the quiet road to her house like she was walking on air. She hated carrying them home. When she used to meet Heidi, she would hump them a few hundred yards to the doctor's surgery and mark the books in their breakout room until Heidi had finished for the day. Now that her best friend was loved up, Freya didn't get that opportunity as much and had to lug the things home. She thought it was fantastic to walk home and carry nothing but her handbag.

"Holy fuck, how many books are in this bag? The strap is cutting into my shoulder."

"Oh, cut your whining. I have to do it every week."

"They're heavy."

"I know," she answered slowly, like he was unable to grasp the concept.

"Can't you get one of those old lady shopping trollies and wheel them home?"

"That's not a bad idea. But you're home now, so you can do all the humping for me."

She gave him a side look to see his reaction. Whenever she mentioned a word linked to sex, his face turned to thunder. There weren't many single women on the island, so he must be getting desperate by now.

"I won't be humping them home for you," he snapped.

Yep, definitely grumpy about something.

"I've spent years lugging my oversized shopping bag with exercise books home, and my shoulders are still intact, no blemishes or lopsided arms."

"It's a wonder you haven't."

"Come on, big strong man like you, afraid of a hundred exercise books?"

"Seems like it. I'd rather give an oil rigger an over-the-shoulder lift while he's passed out drunk than these."

Freya giggled at his grumblings and jogged ahead to her house. She unlocked her front door and held it open for him, then theatrically staggered through the door. He put the bag on the floor, stumbled over to her sofa, and flopped down like he'd run a marathon.

She kicked the door shut with her foot and stood there with her hands on her hips. His hair was the only thing she could see, the arm and the back of the sofa obscuring the rest of him.

"Will you be okay down here while I shower and change quickly?" she called over.

She got a groan as a reply, so she ran up the stairs and got washed and changed. Ten minutes later, she was back down to the living room to find Luke wasn't there.

"Luke," she shouted.

"Up here," he called back.

"What are you doing up there?"

"Reading all your secrets," he replied.

His voice sounded far away and muffled. Then it dawned on Freya where he was. Running back up the stairs two at a time, she hurried down the corridor, past her open bedroom door, the bathroom, and onto the spare room. Sitting on the floor with his ankles crossed and his arms folded was Luke staring up at the wall. He leaned against an armchair. Freya kept the curtains drawn in that room, so nothing faded.

"What are you doing in here? You're supposed to be exhausted from carrying exercise books."

Luke's eyes scanned the wall, and she cringed.

"I got bored," He said, like he was distracted.

"I was ten minutes."

"More like twenty. I got bored after ten minutes and came snooping when there wasn't anything sweet to eat in the kitchen."

"You didn't look hard enough. There was a box of Jason's chocolate chip cookies behind the coffee mugs."

"There was?"

"Yeah. Serves you right for doing a bloke look rather than a woman look."

"Stop side-tracking me with cookies. What the fuck is all of this?"

"Nothing. Come on, let's go," Freya said, mortified that he had seen the room.

"I can't believe you kept everything," he muttered, not moving an inch.

"Didn't you keep mine?" she asked.

"Nah, tossed them as soon as I read them."

That comment shot into her heart like he'd pulled the trigger of a gun.

"What?" she whispered, holding back the tears of his dismissive remark.

"Committed them to memory, of course, but I can't lug around all your letters when I travel the world, and if I'd left them on the rig, then the other shift would've read them. There was no way they were reading about the first time you slept with a man."

"Luke," she snapped.

He ignored her and rose to his feet so fluidly he looked like a dancer the way he moved. On the wall opposite where he was sitting was a map of the world, six feet wide and three feet high. It was mounted on a wooden frame with spongy cork behind the map. Luke moved forward and pressed the different coloured pins. He traced the thin wool strands to mark the various routes he'd made every time he'd gone travelling with his brothers and sister.

"What do these numbers on the stickers mean?"

"I don't want to tell you," Freya said.

She felt stupid for keeping every letter and postcard he'd sent her. She felt ridiculous, marking every journey he'd made and tagging where his favourite places were. Places he'd said he wanted to take her because he thought she'd want to see it. Freya hadn't ever left the UK, although she'd always had a passport. So she felt foolish when she renewed it, hoping Luke would ask her to join him on his set of three weeks off when they coincided with her school holidays. But he never did. The four Turner siblings were closer than any family members she'd met.

Luke turned towards her and then froze. She mustn't have hidden her expression of hurt quickly enough.

"I'm sorry, Freya. I'm not making fun. I really love that you've done this."

It wasn't him pointing out what she'd saved that hurt. It was that he hadn't saved her words. She wrote to him twice when he was on the rigs during his three weeks on and then waited for his letters and postcards when he was on his three weeks off. She'd sent the letters telling him everything that had happened on the island since the previous letter and sealed the back with a kiss. The lipstick she was wearing would stain the back of the envelope. He never answered the questions she'd asked in a letter with his next letter because they rarely arrived in order, so she needed to piece together what she'd asked with his replies. She kept a copy when she wrote him a letter, so they were all in order.

"It's all right. We should get going to search while it's daylight."

"What do the numbers mean, Freya?"

"They log which postcard or letter you sent from overseas. There aren't many from the rigs, so they're in a separate box."

"You have boxes of my letters?"

"Look, Luke, maybe we should go ancestor matching another night. I have a lot to mark, and I could do with getting started."

"Freya," he said, coming right up to her and cupping her shoulders. "I'm sorry I made fun of you for keeping the letters. Where are the boxes?"

She couldn't keep the glum expression off her face and nodded to the wardrobe over in the corner next to the window with the curtains drawn.

He gave her a warning look to silently ask for permission to go and look, and she nodded. His hand slipped down her arm, and he clutched onto her fingers so he could drag her over to the wardrobe. Then, with his free hand, he opened the doors and gasped.

"Holy fuck," he whispered.

Still holding her hand, he opened the drawer at waist level and pulled it out. Stacks of envelopes and single cards were neatly stacked. The top edge was perfectly sliced to lift out the letter inside. Freya tried to pull away, but he squeezed her hand in warning. She relaxed without him looking at her. He lifted an envelope out, and then placed it on top of the stack. Luke chuckled at his scrawl on the front. Picking it up, he squinted at the faded postmark.

"Vienna," she whispered.

"You know which letter this is?"

"Yeah, you met a girl you fell madly for. She took you to the opera. It was your first time."

Luke could hear the sadness and gave her a sharp look.

"I don't remember her name," he muttered.

"Dita."

"Jesus," he whispered.

"Does this feel creepy to you? I can box all this up if it freaks you out," she said, moving to put the letter back in the correct place.

She closed the drawer slowly and quietly with the palm of her hand, then pushed the wardrobe doors shut. With one hand, Luke wasn't grasping tightly.

"No, I'm not creeped out. I feel honoured you kept these, my words and thoughts. I poured everything into those letters. They were my escape to tell you what I was feeling, the thoughts I couldn't share with my siblings because they were hurting as much as I was."

"You know it wasn't your fault, right?"

"I should've been able to do something," Luke said.

He was so quiet as he spoke.

"But you know deep down you couldn't have saved your dad. It was an impossible task. The aneurism was swift."

"Not everyone believes that."

"The only person I care about believing it is you, Luke Turner."

Luke yanked her, so she collided with his chest and wrapped his arms around her in a bear hug. She knew it was the only way not to look at her face and crumble. It was the only way to hide his feelings from her and for that day when his dad died. They stood there for a beat or two until Freya wrapped her arms around his waist and burrowed closer, snuggling in like she was absorbing his pain. She had no idea how much she had done from the moment his mum left to right then. She was always there to share his pain. Even if he was unwilling to let it go. Freya had told him many times that she wanted to take his hurt and throw it into the ocean.

If only that was possible.

"Come on, let's go grave hopping," Freya said.

She lifted her head back, kissed his sternum over his top and shimmied out of his arms. She took his hand and tugged him out of the room.

Luke waited for Freya to lock up, and then he carted her bag to the buggy, making fun that the cart would tip over from the weight of the books. He made a play to put the books on both sides for equal distribution of weight like they were on a boat and could possibly capsize. They made it safely to his cottage, and he was fiddling with the back door key to let them in.

"I can't believe I'm actually going inside your place. You call it a cottage, right?"

"My family call it a cottage, more like a large house. Too big for just me. But Daisy decided we'd all take a cottage instead of taking a room at Edward Hall, and we were to live in age order. So I have Sabrina Lodge."

"It's all weird. You call it a cottage. It's named a lodge but really is a very big house."

Luke finally got the door open, refusing to put the bag down and swung the door open.

"I think the lodge reference comes from when great-grandfather would have all his cronies come to stay, and they would go out hunting. Calling them hunting lodges. They're named after the women in the family. Sabrina is my great-great-great-grandmother, I think. I don't know, really. I should if we're to do the family tree right."

"There must be a scroll somewhere in the library or the study with all your ancestors handwritten in old English."

Luke laughed at her description.

"I'm sure there is, but getting Aunt Cynthia to let us in anywhere in Turner Hall is a feat. We've only entered the study when we were given Edward Hall and these cottages."

"Do you hate it all?"

"I have mixed feelings. All of this grandiose allows us to live and work together. We've only ever known living together, sticking together, warding off the evil aunt and travelling. I don't think we've ever felt settled. I hope when Daisy comes back, we'll start to feel happier. When Daisy returns, it will be around the time Archer and Erica's baby will be born, so we'll be aunts and uncles. That kid is going to be so spoiled."

"I hope Heidi gets the bond back with Keith. I missed him before all this heartache happened with Jason. He's slowly getting there. Sunday dinners are much happier than they were before."

"When do I get an invitation to the dinner table?"

"My mum would have you there every week if you'd

come. You don't need to be invited. Jason and Heidi come every other Sunday, so you can choose to come when they're there or when they're not. I'll be there every Sunday."

"All right, I'll be there."

Freya didn't get further than the open-plan kitchen. But she was there long enough to see the pottery. It sat in the middle of the island. At some stage, it had been coloured a light orange with a peach painted on the side.

"Luke," she said.

Luke didn't put the lights on. He dumped her bag of books and tugged her out of the cottage, locking up far more quickly, and they were on their way to the graveyard. Luke pulled out several pieces of paper from his back pocket and handed them to her. He then took a pen from his other pocket and handed it to her.

"You have pretty writing. Best you fill in the blanks," Luke said with a wide grin.

"Thanks," she said. "I can't remember how many graves there are in the family plot."

"Not that many, less than fifty. My family lost a lot of children in infancy, and I don't know where they were buried. It's only adults, as far as I know."

"That's sad. I hope they were buried somewhere safe."

"I think they were buried in the main church cemetery. We might need to visit there too."

"Okay, let's do this first."

They spent a few hours walking around the overgrown graveyard. Every time Freya looked across at Luke crouched by a gravestone, he was already looking at her. It made her warm all over. She had to put thoughts of Luke out of her head, he had set her in the friends-only box, and she had to live with that. She wouldn't accept it, but she would live with it. It just made it really difficult to concentrate when he was staring at her.

"Can I ask you a question?"

"Anything."

"Why isn't there any furniture in your cottage?"

"I'm not there for long. Either I'm at Edward Hall or my brothers' homes. I haven't been back long."

"Don't you have any personal stuff?"

"A lot of my personal stuff is at the other house. Well, it's in storage, ready to come down here when I can arrange it. I'm going to use the furniture from there. Everything that was in the cottage has been shifted to Edward Hall. I didn't want any of it in the cottage. I know the bed is brand new, so I kept that."

"Why?"

"You know why."

"Is it hard for you to come back?"

"Yeah, really fucking hard. But you're here, and my brothers and sister are here, well Daisy will be here. We all grew up around misery, so it's easier to cope. Misery likes company, I guess."

"Do I make it easier for you?"

Luke stood from his crouched position and came striding over to her. He was so fast that she dropped the paper and pen when he hugged her. He squeezed her so tight the wind got knocked out of her. Freya managed to stretch out her fingers that were squashed between them and flatten them on his chest. He wasn't letting go, not that she wanted him to. Resting her cheek on her hands, she let out a long sigh.

"I don't know what I would do if you weren't here. I'm not convinced I'd stay in the crappy job Archer has given me if you weren't here."

"Luke," she whispered. "I'm not going anywhere."

"Then neither am I."

Luke held onto her so tightly when he stepped away, she swayed. To steady her, Luke lifted his hand to her cheek and stared down at her.

"I feel like I took you for granted all those years I was travelling. I'm not sure I deserve you as a friend, let alone anything else."

Freya froze at the look on Luke's face. What did he mean, let alone anything else? She cleared her throat and crouched, losing his touch and picked up the paper and pen.

"So, do we have everyone plotted?" Luke asked, clearly wanting to change the subject.

Freya wanted to question him further but knew from old that if Luke didn't want to talk about it, no coaxing would work.

"It seems so. All the boxes have names except the two blank gravestones."

"We'll have to check out the leaves on the website and see what connections they've come up with. What if my grandfather had other children we don't know about? Their parties here were raucous by all accounts."

"But he's been dead a while. Why would those graves appear in the last year or so?"

"No idea, but I want to get to the bottom of it. Someone must know."

"I bet Cynthia does."

"I am not going to ask her anything. She won't tell me the truth if her life depended on it."

"I wonder why she's so hateful. Someone must have done her some damage when she was younger."

"My grandfather wasn't all that loving. Not that I'm making excuses for her behaviour."

Now Freya was itching to change the subject.

"Come on, let's go and eat. I'm starving."

"We might have to steal some of Archer's outside chairs, as the only thing I have to sit on is a bed."

Freya felt her cheeks heat up, and she turned her back on Luke to walk back to the cottages. He quickly caught up with her, slung an arm around her neck, and kissed her temple.

"Super sleuthing like we used to do. I'm feeling better already," Luke said.

"Don't forget florin hunting on Saturday," Freya reminded him.

"Can't wait."

15

Luke

Luke had asked Freya to meet him at Turner Hall kitchens as he was embarrassed by the lack of furniture in his cottage. Archer had humped his outdoor chairs back to his rear patio area, leaving him with a wonky wooden stool he remembered seeing in Ralph's shed. He needed to speak to Maggie to ask her a favour.

When he reached the rear of Jason's place, he and Heidi were sitting quietly, reading and sipping on coffee. He took a detour and approached their patio area.

"Hey guys," Luke said as he walked up to the low wall. Heidi was sprawled on one sofa, and Jason was on another. They faced each other with a long coffee table between them with a coffee pot and a plate of pastries.

Luke zoned in on the breakfast pastries.

"Hey Luke, how're things?" Heidi asked.

"They're good. I've got a few things to sort out, and then I'm meeting Freya over in the kitchens."

"Anything we can help with?"

"Are you two portable?"

"We have legs," Jason answered.

"Yes, but are you willing to move from those seats?"

"Yeah. I had to go down to Archer's place to steal their coffee, so I'm not glued to this seat."

"That's one of the things I want to talk about. Are they up and about, or did you help yourself to their kitchen?"

"They're up. Erica was chatting to her stomach twenty minutes ago, and Archer was looking at her like she'd lost her mind."

"Sounds like normal. It's good for the baby to hear their voices," Heidi said.

"Do you need help to carry anything?" Luke asked.

"Absolutely not. I want these pastries to make it to next door," Jason grumbled.

"Damn, they look good too."

"Give him a pastry. There's another ten in the kitchen," Heidi said, laughing.

Sighing dramatically, Jason slouched into the kitchen and brought out a tin, and they were on the move. Erica and Archer were sharing a loveseat, with her head in his lap and her legs over the arm of the sofa. Erica was chattering away while Archer stroked her belly with one hand and held a paperback up in the other hand.

"Stop stealing my stuff, Luke," Archer said without looking up. "I'm fed up with traipsing down to your cottage to fetch it all back."

"That's why I'm here. The stuff from the house will come next week."

"It's about time. Is Daisy okay with that?"

"Daisy organised the shipping."

"Figured you'd delegate," Archer said.

"She's good at that shit," Luke said.

"Luke," Erica admonished. "The baby will learn your dirty swear words before they're born."

"That baby will learn to swear words quicker than you can count to ten. We're oil riggers. No escaping dirty swears Mrs Hollywood," Luke warned.

Erica grinned at him. She pulled her shirt down over her bare bump and covered her belly button with her thumb.

"If his or her first words are shit, I'm blaming you," Erica replied.

Luke rocked back on his heels. "If that's his or her first words, then I'll take the hit and be a super proud uncle."

Archer sighed heavily at the direction o the conversation. "When will the stuff arrive?"

"Next week, Daisy has it all arranged. Then, it will magically appear like it walked itself here."

"Any closer to working out who is buried under the unmarked stones?" Jason asked.

"Kinda yes, kinda no. Will wait for a few more answers first. I'm off florin hunting with Freya, and we might come across other Turner secrets buried in the rocks."

"All the secrets we need to know are in that study. I bet she has a secret door to a hidden room where all the Turner scandals are hidden away," Jason said.

"Nah, all the Turner secrets are hidden in her rooms. That's why we're not allowed in there," Archer said.

"Probably. Anyway, how is it going with Freya? Resolved the mystery over the engagement ring?" Erica asked.

"I gotta go," Luke said, stuffing his face with a pastry.

He didn't want to answer any questions about Freya until he knew her feelings. There was no chance of a kiss the night she was marking books in his empty kitchen because she fell asleep on the floor with a book open on her lap. He felt bad about the conditions he put her through, even with feeding her. So he took her home and gave her a head kiss like he usually did.

He could hear Jason's cackle and Archer calling him a pussy. Then he heard Erica chastise him. Laughter broke out and faded as he jogged to the kitchens and, hopefully, Freya.

Coming to the open doorway, he squinted into the dark kitchen from the bright summer's day. He couldn't see anyone for a few seconds, and then his eyes adjusted. Freya sat at the kitchen table on the bench with her hands around a Turner sibling mug. She was grinning at something Maggie was saying. Maggie was at the stove chattering away, waving a spatula in the air as she spoke. Luke found it remarkable that every generation of Maggie's family had stood in that kitchen, and the same for Bailey's family. Ralph's father and grandfather had taken care of the grounds. But the irony wasn't lost on him that he also had come back to continue the Turner family line, even though it was Archer's role to produce an heir. Walking through the family tree with Freya brought to light the starkness that he and his siblings were the only row on the family tree to still live.

"Hi, Maggie," Luke said, walking into the kitchen when Bailey clocked him, standing in the corner with a tiny tea cup.

"Luke," she cried out. "Come here and give this old lady a hug."

Luke grinned at her and wrapped her in a tight hug. "You're far from old Maggie."

"Tell my bones that," she said and chuckled, cupping his

cheek to pat once. "Take a seat next to Freya, and I'll get you some breakfast."

"Is there any coffee on the go?"

"No, but there is tea in the pot. Freya got you a mug ready," Maggie said.

"Did you now?" Luke said to Freya.

He plonked himself on the bench next to her, hooked an arm around her neck and kissed her head.

"Morning," he said.

"Morning, Luke. Are you ready for today's adventure?"

"Oh Lord, where are you two off to today?" Maggie said, turning to look at them.

"Florins," Luke said.

"There are no florins on this island. The Turners settled centuries after the florins you're after were in circulation. That's just a rumour. There are no boxes of Italian florins here on the island. I bet that was floated at the card table when they were betting the island as an extra incentive," Bailey said good-naturedly.

"All rumour starts with an element of truth, doesn't it?" Freya asked Bailey.

"Yes, that is true," Bailey boomed in his low tenor, but if there was any here, I'm sure Luke's great-great-great-grandfather would've found them. He documented the entire island. Every nook and cranny.

"It's a shame those maps are not in existence anymore."

"But they are," Maggie said enthusiastically.

Bailey cleared his throat, and they all looked at him as if he was subtly shaking his head. "The Mistress won't let them be made public. Jennifer has tried for years to let them be put on display at the museum to show how the island looked back then, but she won't allow it."

"We were mapping the graveyard. I have so many questions like, what are the odds that all first children were male. We went back ten generations, and all firstborns were male. Until Frederick and Cynthia, only the firstborn survived, passed thirty. There are no cousins, not even removed or long lost watered-down Turners," Freya said.

"As far as I know, many died in wars over the centuries. The crown sent our men all over the world to fight our wars. No one has ever accused the Turner men of cowardice. They went off to war and did their duty, and sadly, many didn't come back. The girls seemed to have not survived infancy or childhood. Some never married, of course, but yes, it is sad that there are not more Turners filling this grand hall."

Bailey's face fell for a moment, and then he sipped his tea.

"Well," Freya said brightly. "Archer is married with a baby on the way. Jason is married. I imagine they'll start a family soon. Then there is Luke. He won't be single for long, I imagine. Daisy, I don't know her well, so I can't say. Do you want kids, Luke?" Freya asked, looking his way.

"Yeah, I want a big family if my wife is willing."

"If she's willing?"

"Well, you can't help who you fall in love with, so if she didn't want children, I would accept it."

"Wow," Freya said.

"It's good to hear this Turner generation is more modern," Maggie said. "If your grandfather were alive, he would have something else to say about that," Maggie said.

"What could he do?" Luke asked.

No one would dictate who he would marry.

"He was of his time, let's say. He chose who married who, and no one argued. If they did, there were severe consequences," Maggie said.

"Like what?" Freya asked, leaning forward, almost whispering.

She grinned at the potential gossip coming from Maggie.

"I couldn't say," she replied, giving Freya a wink.

"That sounds like a won't to me," Freya said, clapping her hands. "Does it have anything to do with the blank gravestones?"

"I don't know anything about that," Maggie said, dropping any humour.

Freya looked at Luke and raised her eyebrows, silently conveying that it was ominous.

"Okay, who wants what?" Maggie asked, looking between Luke and Freya.

"Scrambled eggs on toast and bacon," Freya said.

"Me too, Maggie. Do you need us to do anything?"

Maggie watched Bailey leave and then looked over to Luke. "Looks like you'll need to get your own cutlery, and that tea might need a top-up of hot water."

"Where's Bailey off to?"

"Gone to do an errand for me. He'll be back soon."

Ten minutes later, Bailey came back wheeling a sack trolley with four recognisable boxes. Luke groaned, knowing what was in them.

"Maggie," Luke hissed at her like a child.

"What's in the boxes?" Freya asked, chirpy as ever.

"Nothing," Luke said.

"All your letters," Maggie replied to Freya.

"All my letters? You said you tossed them," Freya said, now sporting a scowl.

"Ha! Tossed them. I don't know who told you that, but these have been preserved like they were ancient documents. All are sealed in bags so they don't fade or get water damaged. Luke was worried they'd go mouldy in an old house like this."

Freya took a slow glance between the boxes by the far door to the outside and back to Luke. He sat there sheepish about being called out on his lie.

"Okay, so I lied. Happy now?" Luke said, holding out his hands.

Maggie chose that moment to place their food in front of them. Luke was grateful for the distraction, knowing Freya never chatted while she ate. He had at least five minutes before the questions came.

"Thanks, Maggie. Can I leave them by the door until we come back from florin hunting?"

"I'll get Ralph to come with his lawnmower he sits on. He can attach the trailer and take them to your back door."

"I can't have you do that stuff just for me," Luke protested.

"Sure you can. Now that he has Keith helping him, he's looking to do more. You have to understand you're a Turner, Luke. We are here to take care of you, however, that might be. Lugging four boxes across to Sabrina lodge is no hardship, just like making your breakfast isn't a hardship. I'm happy to do it, and so is Ralph."

"If there is anything you need me to do for you, you only need to say the word, Luke. Maggie and I feel like we're your second parents, and we want to help wherever we can," Bailey said.

"That's so sweet," Freya whispered and then sniffed.

Luke was lost for words. He'd spent so much time away from Turner Hall and hating Cynthia so much he'd forgotten there were good people at Turner Hall.

"You know what would make me really happy?" Maggie asked.

"What's that?"

"Babies. Make lots of babies that we can cherish," she said.

"I need to find a girl first that isn't daunted by all of this. Then I have to convince her to marry me," Luke said.

"I'm sure you'll find a way to make that happen," Maggie replied.

Luke couldn't help looking at Freya. She was already staring at him, expressionless, but there was a warmth to her eyes he couldn't miss.

"Eat up. We need to get going if we're going to beat the tide," Luke said.

Freya snapped out of her trance but didn't hide her smug grin. They ate quietly and quickly, then as soon as the last mouthful was swallowed, Luke was up and grabbed Freya's hand, hauling her out of the kitchen and shouting his thanks to Maggie. Luke didn't miss Freya rubbernecking the four boxes at the door and giving the top one a pat before they left.

Luke didn't speak until they reached the fencing at the top of the path leading down to the private beach. When he tugged on her hand, Freya was about to start the trek down.

"What?" she said, lifting her hand to shield her eyes from the sunshine.

"Do you think Maggie and Bailey know who is buried under the blank stones?"

"Undoubtedly."

"Do you think they'll ever say?"

"Not while Cynthia is alive. I bet it's like a prime minister thing. Archer will be handed the key to the cupboard of Turner secrets, and then it will be too late to ask any questions," Freya said.

"Do you think that's kind of sad?"

"Heartbreaking. Granny keeps telling Heidi, me, and Keith to ask her all the questions now before she loses her marbles or dies. She bangs on about the family, knowing where they came from and who their family are. It seems like who the Turners are is shrouded in mystery. Either there is nothing to know, and we're in a Wizard of Oz situation, or the truth is so sad and heart-wrenching we're being saved from it all to the point when we know we must accept it."

"We?" Luke asked. Buoyed by the notion, she might be contemplating a relationship with him.

"I'll always be your best friend, Luke. I'll see you through whatever heartache comes your way."

"Freya," he said with a sigh, bringing her in for a hug.

"Don't get all sappy on me now, Luke Turner. You're gruff and brusque and indifferent, telling lies to avoid showing your soft side."

"I have never lied to you."

"I tossed your letters," she said, trying to mimic his voice.

"Apart from that," he said.

"Anything else you're keeping from me?"

Luke was about to say no, but that would be a lie. He was keeping from her that he wanted to be more than best friends. With her so close, smelling like she did of peaches, comfort and woman, he wanted to confess everything he was feeling about her, even if he couldn't figure it all out.

Instead, he said, "Let's go hunting."

Luke took off at a jog, leaving her at the top of the path, huffing out a telling-off he couldn't hear over the screeching seagulls. He cupped his hand at his ear and shook his head as he ran backwards down the track. Luke turned, so he didn't fall over a boulder and sprinted the rest of the way, expanding the distance between them. He needed to get his wits together in case he showed her exactly how he was feeling. And he wasn't ready for rejection.

He slowed as soon as he hit the sand, and Freya caught up with him a few minutes later.

16

Luke

Luke left his cottage and headed to Edward Hall. The world champion rowing team had arrived at the hall the previous evening, and he had greeted them when they had dinner. Luke wanted to make sure they'd settled well and had everything they needed. Moving quickly across the lawns, he spotted Archer and Freya standing at the stone balustrade overlooking Edward Hall lawns that had been converted to an outdoor exercise area. He knew why Archer was there but not why Freya was there, especially when it was a school day.

He was disappointed they didn't find anything in the cove, but there was all summer to look.

He could hear her chattering away in her breathy voice. As Luke neared, he saw what had her in a trance. All the rowing team were in gym trainers, gym shorts and nothing else, racing up and down in lines.

"I mean, Archer, if any of them need a medic—"

Luke cut in. "I will be going to their rescue."

Freya spun on the spot. She was in tailored black shorts cut off mid-thigh with an oversized grandad shirt, and a flimsy top underneath that showed off the curves of her breasts. She had black plimsolls with no socks.

Her cheeks were pinked beautifully.

"Hi, Luke," she said. "What are you doing here?"

"It's my job to be here. I thought your job was at a school where kids are taught by teachers like you. You look gorgeously healthy, so you're not sick. So tell me, Peaches, why are you here ogling the rowing team?"

"Inset day," she mumbled.

"Come again?"

"It's an inset day. Teacher training day."

"And salivating over the rowing team is part of the curriculum?"

Luke didn't know where his snippiness had come from. He could usually control it when Freya looked at other men, but then he was his own worst enemy. If he made a move to see how she felt, then he wouldn't have to bite her head off every time hot men were running around Edward Hall.

"We start later on an inset day. I had an hour to spare before I needed to head into school."

"Your school is a three-minute walk from where you live. Here," he said, pointing to the lawns. "Is a buggy ride away."

"I wanted to see Heidi?" she posed it as a question, making Archer laugh openly.

"I'm sure the rowing team don't want women gazing at them half naked while they're training."

"I don't mind," one of the men shouted up from below them on the grass where one of the markers was sticking out of the ground.

"Oh, hi, Pete. How's it going?" Freya called out.

"Pete," Luke hissed through his teeth so Pete couldn't hear. "You know his fucking name?"

"Yeah, they were in town last night to get a bite to eat. I bumped into them on my way home."

"Are you still on for a drink tonight?" Pete shouted up.

"No," Luke called out.

"Sure," Freya replied, not looking at Pete but smirking at Luke with her arms folded under her breasts and her eyebrow raised. She moved from side to side, goading him to say more.

"I'll be in the pub at eight. See you there," Freya said, and Pete jogged away.

"He's not going to pick you up? What kind of guy doesn't pick up his girl for a date?"

"You know everyone can hear your yelling, don't you?" Jason said, coming up onto the balcony. "I can practically hear you from the kitchens."

Luke dropped his head back and looked at the cloudless sky. He might as well declare his love for Freya right there with his lack of subtlety.

"I know you're protective of me, and I love you for it. But I am a grown-up and can drink with anyone I want. It's just a drink," Freya said.

"He wasn't looking at you like he just wanted a drink, Peaches," Luke bit out.

"So?" she said, shrugging a shoulder. "I gotta get to work. I'll see you at Sunday lunch?"

"Yeah," Luke said sullenly. "One o'clock."

"All right then. Bye Luke, Jason, Archer." Then she turned to the rowing team and bellowed out, "Bye, team."

Luke stood fuming as the entire team stopped what they were doing and shouted back their goodbyes. Jesus fuck, she had hoards of men after her.

"When are you going to pull your head out of your arse?" Jason commented once Freya was out of hearing range.

"I don't know what you're talking about," Luke said, failing to take the childish tone out of his words.

"Man, if you don't make a move soon, there are twenty guys out there who will. And that is just this morning. She waltzed out here, and all of them, even the married ones, stopped their exercises and just stared. Their drill sergeant had to snap them out of their daze," Archer said.

"I don't know what to do."

"Just kiss her," Archer said.

"Have you heard of consent?" Luke asked.

"Erica did that to me," Archer said.

"Oh yes, pot, you resisted kissing her for like ages."

"Well, kettle, we kissed, and now we're married. Just saying," Archer said a little too smugly.

"All right, kids, play nicely. I need to get back and take the pastries out of the oven," Jason said, patting them both on the back.

"Save me one," Luke shouted out without turning.

Luke looked out across the lawn at the men working out, knowing full well any of them would jump at the chance of a drink with Freya, not just Pete and not just because of her heart-shaped bottom. She was everything a man could want.

"Why am I C&B manager?" Luke asked.

"That was the role divvied up for you. That's what you went back to college to study," Archer replied evenly.

"So it's not because you don't trust me?"

"What the hell are you talking about, brother? I'd trust you with my life."

"Just not the client's lives," Luke replied quietly.

"What did she say?" Archer clipped out. "Cynthia. What did she say to you?"

"It doesn't matter."

"Yes, it fucking does. Jason, Daisy, and me. We all trust you. What happened that day was not your fault. When we had to divide this venture, it never occurred to offer endurance courses or space for athletes to come and train in privacy. We thought we would be doing weddings."

"What happens if they need a medic?"

"You know they've got one with them. He's sitting over there on a log. You met him, Luke."

"I feel so useless, Archer. My role here just seems artificial."

"You've only been back a month or so. It takes a while to assimilate into island life again. I struggled until I married Erica. You'll find your groove. But get Cynthia out of your head. She is poison and is hell-bent on making everyone else as miserable as she is."

"I'll try."

"If you're in love with Freya, you should tell her. If she doesn't love you back, then you can move on. But don't make her wait, just in case she does love you. We know how life can end in a flash."

"All right," Luke said quietly.

"Luke," Archer snapped in the only way a big brother could.

"I'll tell her, kiss her, whatever, by the end of the weekend. I'll make a move, and we'll see."

"Good. If she does love you, then get married, don't fuck about. Let's start making our own families up at the cottages and bring happiness back to these halls and fuck Cynthia Turner. Let her have the main house. The cottages and plenty big enough for us."

"Right. On that note, do you think I'd be allowed to get into the study? Or is it only the eldest allowed in there?"

Archer pulled a set of keys out of his pocket and twisted off a key.

"That will let you in. I'm sure Bailey won't bar the way if you have a key. All I ask is that it's only you that goes in there. Let it just be family for now. I haven't had time to look around, and while I trust Freya, if there are deep dark secrets in there, I'd rather know first."

"That's a deal. I'm looking for old maps of the island. Bailey said our great-great-great-grandfather mapped the whole island, and Cynthia won't hand them over to the museum."

"Are you still looking for those florins?"

"Yep. If there are florins and the whereabouts are known, even if it's a clue, I can't imagine Cynthia would leave them in that study. When Dad died, we had to go back to the rigs after the funeral. She had all the time in the world to hide away anything of interest."

"I'm hoping she doesn't know what she's looking for, seeing as she was stripped of her inheritance and only gained it when Dad died. Her father would have been too elderly to care."

"She cares. If there is any chance something might allude to money, you can bet she had stuffed it under her mattress."

Luke laughed at the picture Archer was painting.

"Seriously, Brother, if you're miserable in the role of conference and banqueting manager, we'll find another place for you where you are happy. I don't want you to regret coming home."

"Okay, thanks, Archer. I better get to the office before

Stan has a fit if I'm not answering the phone. I do not want a spanner on my desk."

"That is the truth. I think Jason will have words if he produces another spanner from his coat pocket."

"That was so funny. Right, I'm off, see you later," Luke said, strolling away with his hands in his pockets, wondering if he could go through with what he'd told Archer he would do.

Confessing to Freya how he felt was monumental, but he didn't see a way forward unless he told her and found out how she felt about him.

17

Freya

When Freya had an inset day, it was bliss. A later alarm clock, a casual stroll to work, getting comfy in the staff lounge with her colleagues, and then getting to work setting up her plans for the new term. Her day started spectacularly watching the rowing team exercise on the lawns. Heidi had tipped her off but made it clear she was staying in bed so she could gawp on her own. Ten minutes after she arrived to watch, this time without her blow-up chair, Archer joined her at the balustrade. He handed her a freshly made coffee. The coffee came via Jason, whose wife told him to get a cup to her while she watched. She loved her friends like they were her family. She'd hitched a lift with her brother Keith who was helping Ralph erect some kind of apparatus for the boys to practice on down at the beach. She'd walk back to school as she had plenty of time.

Bumping into Luke was a lovely surprise, especially

seeing him in his suit trousers, shirt and scowling face. Why he was moody, she was checking out the guys she'd never know. Freya hoped he wouldn't turn into an overbearing best friend even though he didn't want her romantically. He'd made that clear with the reaction to her engagement ring. She fiddled with it as she sat at her school desk, sifting through her notebooks for the following term's timetable, when her head teacher, Dudley Morris, came strolling in.

"I hope you're making good use of your time today, Ms Riley. If you don't have enough to do, I can always give you extra work."

Mr Morris had been surly for weeks. It was like he honed into her happiness about Luke returning for good and then let loose on causing her stress at work. The number of after-school classes he made her take. Lunchtime sessions meant she had to eat her lunch in six and a half minutes otherwise, she would have to function on coffee, and she had done that too many times to know it wouldn't work. It had been full-on all term, staying late every night to cover each staff member that called in sick. As the only single teaching staff member, Mr Morris decided she was the best fit to cover, and it would look good on her CV for future roles. Freya wasn't planning on leaving the school until she retired. If she never got promoted, then so be it. She loved teaching. So why he thought she needed to beef up her CV, she didn't know. But she understood the logic that she had no one to go home to, where the other teachers had families. She didn't question why he didn't cover as his children had long since flown the nest, and his wife divorced him years ago. He was the head teacher, as he often reminded her when she asked pointed questions. Working late meant the morning jaunt up to Edward

Hall was the first time she had seen Luke all week, making her grumpy. Especially after learning he'd kept her letters after all.

"I think I've done my fair share this term, Mr Morris. Covering everyone else's classes after school. Supervising the martial arts class was interesting, seeing as I've never done that skill before."

She couldn't help her sarcasm and winced internally, knowing she'd regret the outburst.

"A school is for learning, Ms Riley. Hopefully, you've learned something this term."

"Was there a particular lesson you wanted me to focus on?" she asked.

His hidden meaning was lost on her because he was definitely hinting at something.

"Don't play the fool," he replied.

Just as he turned, Luke came skidding to a stop at her classroom door. He was holding a familiar bag.

"Luke Turner. I never thought I'd see you back here. You didn't much enjoy it the first time around."

"I think you'll find, despite your constant bullying, I had full attendance," Luke replied.

The penny dropped, and her skin went clammy. Was Mr Morris being mean to her because she was best friends with Luke Turner? What did Luke do to Mr Morris?

"I shall have to check the records," Mr Morris replied.

"Unless they've removed it, you don't have to. My name is engraved on the honour roll in the main hall," Luke clipped out.

No one liked being called a liar, but Luke hated it.

Freya could see the fury rolling off Mr Morris. His spine went straighter then his hands fisted at his sides. He turned his upper body and looked at Freya.

"You'd better make this quick. I don't pay you to talk to a Turner."

He stalked off. Freya watched as Luke narrowed his eyes on her boss as he marched down the corridor, his shoes clipping at a fast pace.

"Does he still have a stick up his arse?" Luke said, coming into the classroom.

He swung the padded lunch bag on his fingers as he came closer and sat on the corner of her desk. She thought he was so handsome with his tousled hair and gorgeous brown eyes.

"He's been a nightmare for a while. Since you returned, I'd say. What's his beef with you?"

"I've no idea. None of us would put up with Mr Morris' bullying, so much so we never really talked about it, just ignored him. I haven't seen him since I left school. I thought he'd retired years ago."

"He leaves at the end of the summer term, and then we get a new head teacher. None of us has met them yet. We don't even know a name."

"Is he giving you hassle? Do you want me to talk to him?"

"No, please don't. It will only make it worse. I have one more term with him, and then the grief will be over, and I can get some sleep over the summer."

"Freya, what is he doing?"

The swinging lunch bag was now thumped onto her desk. She feared for her apple and the bruises it would have. But she knew this version of Luke. He would keep on and on until she gave in and told him. It was the same when she lost her virginity. He wrote to her every day until she wrote him back and told him a name. His letters overlapped with hers, so she had to put up with a dozen letters after she'd sent hers. Then they stopped after the letter that told her he was unimpressed with her choice. He didn't write to her for a month after that.

"He's making me work overtime because there is a sickness bug going around and not enough spare teachers in the evening."

"Is that why you haven't been able to meet in the evenings?"

"Yeah, that's not news, Luke."

"What a dickhead. I'm going to have a chat with him," Luke said, getting up from his perch.

He leaned down, cupped her neck, kissed her head, and squeezed her neck. That was a new move for him. He didn't usually clutch onto her when he kissed her head. Then he was gone. Left in confusion about his mission or if he would come back, she plucked her lunch bag off the table and put it in her desk drawer. She must have left it in the buggy with Keith because she hadn't remembered taking it to the balustrade to watch the men.

An hour later, Mr Morris came back to her classroom. She did a slow blink at the papers in front of her and plastered on a smile when she met his stare.

"Hello, Mr Morris."

"Ms Riley. I've decided I don't need you to cover the year 10 rugby match tomorrow morning."

"That's great to hear, seeing as I didn't know I was supposed to cover it."

"Yes, well, the notice was in the staff room. I guess you've been working in here and hadn't seen it."

"Nope."

Year 10 rugby? She had no idea about rugby apart from the shape of the ball.

"You're not required. Mrs Sloper informed me that she

will be well enough to attend school next week, so she will be covering the evening classes for the week."

"That is good news. Dare I hope I have my evenings back?"

"Yes, Ms Riley."

"Thank you, Mr Morris."

The head teacher nodded his head once and left the open space of her doorway. She sagged in her chair, stretching her legs out under the desk and dropped her arms to the sides. Freya was slowly slipping. She would end up on the floor if she didn't dig her heels into the carpet. She wouldn't mind a nap, but she needed to get on if she was to leave on time to get home, have an actual disco nap, get showered and changed for her drink with Pete.

Freya knew Luke would turn up at some stage. It was like he was focused solely on what she was doing, who she was seeing and where she was every moment of the day. Living on Copper Island meant she couldn't go far, and teaching at the local school meant he knew where she was between eight in the morning and four in the afternoon, then back to the evening.

They knew everything about each other but hadn't spent time together since he left when he was twenty-two for the rigs. That was nine years ago, longer if she counted the time he studied away from Copper Island. Now that they were spending a lot of time together, she wasn't used to the scrutiny but loved that he cared enough to come and check out Pete.

Freya was sitting on a tall stool at the bar next to Pete, with her back to the door. The hellos to Luke had a ripple effect around the busy pub, so she didn't jump when he threw an arm around her neck and kissed her temple. Instead, she sighed and gave an apologetic face to Pete.

"Hey, babe, I thought I'd come for a beer," Luke said casually, not removing his arm and leaning against the arm of the high stool.

Babe? He had never called her babe before, but then he hadn't come searching for her dates. Even when she dated in her late teens, he never came and checked them out. He was too busy on his own dates to care enough.

She sighed long and heavily.

"Pete, this is my best friend, Luke Turner. You've met his brothers, Archer and Jason. They run Edward Hall together. There's another sibling, Daisy, but she's currently off island."

"Yeah, I've known Freya since we were kids. Haven't I, Peaches?" Luke said.

Freya leaned back to get a look at Luke. Was he high?

"Haven't you got someplace to be?" Freya said.

"Nope, let me get you guys a drink," Luke said.

"Look, Freya, it was great chatting with you, but I need to get an early night for training tomorrow. Maybe we can catch up another night?" Pete said.

Pete stood away from his stool and looked at Freya to see how he could wedge himself near her without touching Luke to kiss her goodbye, but he glanced at their proximity and gave up. He necked the last third of his pint and gave them both a wave while he was still swallowing. Then he walked out of the pub.

Luke took his seat and signalled for the bar server to come over.

"Same again," he said, pointing to her empty wine glass.

Freya sighed again. "Might as well, seeing as you've scared off my date."

"If he wasn't man enough to stick around, then he is not right for you."

"You sound like a cliché."

"There is nothing wrong with a cliché if it's right."

They fell into chatter, and before she blinked, it was closing time, and Luke was giving her a piggyback home while she laughed at his awful jokes. He dropped her off at her front door and waited for her to unlock it and step inside.

All humour evaporated when he stepped to the threshold and wrapped his hand around her neck.

"You know, Freya Riley. One of these days, I will tell you exactly the kind of man you need in your life."

"Will it be soon? Because I'm not getting any younger, and I want babies," she said and grinned in his face, swaying into his warm hand.

"Yes, I promise it will be soon," he whispered before kissing her forehead.

Freya felt her stupefied look as she let out a giggle. "Good."

"Shall I come and pick you up in the buggy, or will you come to me?"

"I'll come to you. I want to see Sabrina again and dream of all the things I want to get to put in her to make her a home. I love that cottage so much, and not just because Heidi lives next door."

Freya slumped against the door frame, her eyes lidded with sleep. "I'm so tired. At least next week I don't have to do any evening classes. Mr Morris has let me off the hook. Hey," she said, coming alive again. "Did you have anything to do with that?"

"Don't know what you're talking about. I'm happy you have some free time next week in the evenings. I'll make you dinner, and you can make plans for Sabrina."

"Cool," she said. "I need to get to bed, Luke. See you tomorrow at about ten... ish."

"All right, Peaches. I'll be up," Luke said and kissed her head before he stepped back. "Lock the door."

She gave him a hearty wink, stepped back, closed the door and clicked the latch down. She looked through the peephole to see him looking up at her bedroom window and then walking down the road.

She was drunk but not drunk enough to know something was happening between them. She just didn't know what that was.

18

Luke

Luke sat on a large tea chest, kicking his legs as he ate his breakfast bagel. Next to him Erica ate an apple.

"You're making me feel unhealthy," Luke muttered, side-eyeing Erica's choice of breakfast.

"I'm thirty months pregnant. Everything gives me heartburn. Someone said to try apples. So I'm reluctantly eating an odd-shaped apple from Freya's parent's apple tree."

"Thirty months? Wow that's longer than an elephant. I'd forgotten they had an apple tree. Me and Freya used to steal all the apples and take them down to the coves where we would hunt for treasure. Anyway, you're not anywhere near your due date."

"I feel like I am. Another month or so, and then I get to cuddle him or her."

"I'll be an uncle. How scary is that!"

"You'll be a fabulous uncle. Balance out Jason's gruffness and Archer's seriousness. Daisy will spoil the little one and bring her sunshine to the table."

"Are you nervous?"

"No, strangely calm, like I was always meant to be here and meet Archer. Build a family with him and all of you lot."

"And building up all this, too," Luke said, pointing to the warehouse behind them.

"I know. I'm more nervous about how that will work than bringing a human into the world. I'm an outsider basically telling the residents of Copper Island they need to share their belongings."

"You're thinking of the island, sustainability, carbon footprint. I bet this place will be busy every day."

"Are you going to tell me who you have to help out today?"

"Here they come now," Luke said, pointing to the end of the quay.

Freya, Heidi and six kids were strolling down the concrete path. One kid was on the other side of Freya, and the other five kids were on the other side of Heidi.

"Kids?"

"Yeah. Don't worry. I have their parent's permission, along with the head teacher's agreement. They're going to do detention here every Saturday until the end of term."

"Isn't that Ralph's kid, Kenny?"

"Yep. I found those kids kicking the shit out of him a couple of months ago. Then I found out they were bullying him out of his pocket money because they assumed he had money because Ralph was up at Turner Hall."

"Christ, if only they knew the reality," Erica said, tossing the apple core into a makeshift bin. "Well, I dislike bullies as much as I dislike the casting couch, so let's get them to work."

Luke hopped off the chest and strode towards Freya, hugged her and kissed her cheek.

"Ew, gross, man," the ring leader of the bullies said.

"Button it, kiddo. We spoke about this on the way here. The better you behave, the quicker this will be over. You annoy me, then the pain lasts longer," Freya said, still in Luke's arms.

"I think I might quite like you," Luke said.

"What? You already quite like me, Luke Turner."

"Oh yeah, keep forgetting. Right, this way."

Luke led the boys while Heidi and Freya splintered off to find Erica. Kenny fell into step next to him as they entered the warehouse.

"Why do I have to be here too? I'm quite happy at school with detention," he mumbled.

"Life lessons, mate. You'll learn a lot over these next seven weeks."

Once they were deep into the massive warehouse the size of a football field, he told them to gather around.

"All right. The aim of today is to get as many of the higher boxes down to ground level. They're old, sturdy and can be reused, so there is no throwing them down to the ground. Four of you work in pairs, two on each side and hand them down. One of you will be outside with me sorting through the contents."

"What about Kenny? What's he going to do?" the ring leader asked.

"Kenny is your supervisor. He's going to make sure you work for the next four hours. You'll get a twenty-minute break after an hour and forty-five minutes. They'll be drinks and snacks outside waiting for you. If I hear you giving

Kenny a hard time, then things will get harder because I will make sure things get harder for you. So pick who is coming outside. It doesn't matter who is first, as you'll take a turn outside sorting each week. We reckon there are over a thousand boxes in here. Those on the floor are bigger and can stay where they are. By the end of the seven weeks, this place will be empty, and your time served will be your punishment done."

Not a peep out of the five for a few moments, and then rumblings between them about who would stay and who would go. While they battled it out over rock paper scissors, Luke took Kenny to one side.

"Here is a clipboard with numbers on them. It's supposed to be the inventory to this place, but I don't hold much faith as this was emptied before it was handed to us. On the side of each tea chest is a shipping number. Find it on the list before they hump it outside and tick it off. If the number is not there, they use this spray can, and number it yourself and add it to the sheet. Got that?"

"Yes, Mr Turner."

"Luke's fine, mate. I need to get this place ready before the baby is born, so your assistance in ensuring everything is accounted for will be a big help. Managing people who hate you will always be there in your life. Learn how to manage that now, and then when you get to university and then the workplace, you'll know how to deal with it. Don't be an arsehole."

"Got it."

"Great, give me a shout whenever you find a box with something in it."

"Right."

By the end of the morning and the allotted four hours he put the kids to work, they hadn't cleared a great deal of the warehouse. He was glad now that he'd negotiated seven weeks with the parents and school. He'd offer Kenny evenings when his dad worked late.

The five teenagers ended up working as a team and working hard. He guessed they needed a little direction with something productive to do. Heidi and Freya had headed up to the cottages with Erica, who faked exhaustion. He knew she was faking it when she sat on the back of the golf buggy, wiggling her fingers as they retreated. He didn't care. Living on the island, he hadn't sorted out his routine to work out, so humping boxes all day was perfect exercise.

Kenny came sauntering out of the warehouse with his jumper tied around his waist. His t-shirt was wet from the exertion of directing the others.

"Did you have a good morning?" Luke asked him, handing him a bottle of water.

"I did. When you first told me I had to get them to work, I was ready to sneak out the back. But I didn't want to let you down, and it worked really well in the end."

"How did you manage it?"

"We worked together mapping the warehouse first, sectioning it out so we could achieve our box goal each Saturday."

"That's smart," Luke said. "Good management comes from the top. A good manager makes sure the people they lead are working at their best."

"I think that's the problem with the school," Kenny muttered.

"You don't like Mr Morris?"

"I don't think any kid likes their head teacher, but he's so angry and bitter. For some reason, he truly hates the Turners. I made the mistake of telling him that you helped me with some issues, and he hit the roof. Apparently, I should have gone to him, but he isn't that approachable."

"Well, I had strong words with him to get you all here for seven Saturdays. I'm glad you found it a good experience. I'll see you next Saturday?"

"Yeah, for sure. Look, Luke, I found this tin. No one else saw it. When I was on the top tier looking down, I saw a blanket and a kerosene lamp. It looked like someone was camping out, so I hopped across the boxes to get rid of it in case whoever it was came back. Except it looked girly, and it was wrapped around this tin."

Luke looked down at Kenny's hand and saw a metal-style lunch box. It was dented, with the green paint peeling off, showing the gunmetal grey underneath. If Luke wasn't mistaken, it looked like a military box of some kind.

"Did you open it?" Luke asked, reaching for it.

"It's locked or jammed, but it's heavy, and I can feel things moving inside."

"All right, I'll take a look. Thanks for keeping this quiet. It doesn't look like the junk we've ploughed through today. If you see any more like this next week, give me a shout."

"Sure, Luke. See you next week or around Turner Hall with Dad."

"You need a lift home?"

"Nah, gotta meet my Dad at the chippy, reward for working with you guys."

"Enjoy," Luke said quietly, staring at the box.

He looked up, and Kenny was heading towards the fish shop at the end of the quay. Luke then looked up at the massive warehouse and wondered what other treasures they'd find. Erica had lost her mind over the vintage clothing she found in a suitcase. He wondered if he should check with Cynthia if they could sell what he found in the warehouse. Cynthia had given them the warehouse and its contents, so he figured it was all theirs.

Luke dragged the few boxes they'd used as seats into the siding of the shutter doors and then pulled them closed. After clipping on the padlock, he scooped up the tin and hopped into the golf buggy heading for the cottages.

19

Freya

She opened the back door at ten in the morning like she'd arranged with Luke, but his kitchen was silent. Freya had already passed Archer and Erica's place, and that was silent. Before that, she'd taken a detour to see if hot men were working out, but there was no one at Edward Hall. When she passed Jason and Heidi's place, she heard giggling from the upstairs open window and smiled. Her best friend getting her happy ever after was awesome.

"Luke," she called out.

"Up here," he called back.

Freya walked through the empty rooms on the ground floor. She touched the vase and bowl and then got to the stairs. Taking them two at a time, she walked along the carpeted floor, tutting at nothing in any of the rooms as she passed the open doors until she got to the end. Luke was kneeling on the bed that looked like he'd made it at one point but then decided to have a one-man wrestle on it. He looked at her exasperated, his hair pulled in all directions. Never had he looked more adorable. He gave an unhappy face and extended his hand with the tin.

"Can't get it open," he muttered and collapsed onto the bed.

Freya climbed onto the mattress, not hiding her laughter, as she grabbed hold of the tin and shook it like she was trying to guess a birthday present.

"What's in here?"

"I don't know. It looks like a WWII soldier's tin. There could be anything in there."

Freya turned it around, looking for clues but found nothing but peeling paint. She fell to her back and lifted it above her head like a different angle would help her.

"Should we try to pick the lock?" Freya suggested.

"Do you know how to pick a lock?"

"I had to do it once when I lost my key to my journal. The internet will tell us how to unpick this particular lock. They'll probably have videos too."

"Well, let's leave the breaking-in until later. I want to get to that cove again and see if the glint I saw was actually a florin or another old coin."

"All right then, do you promise to work on more of the family tree stuff? I'm addicted to all those leaves popping up," Freya said.

"Have you been sneaking a look behind my back?" Luke asked with a grin, tickling her sides.

Freya let out a guffaw and wriggled off the bed. "No, I swear, but I know there will be answers."

"Fine. Have you eaten?"

"Yes, have you?"

"Yes, nuked porridge because Jason and Archer weren't up."

"If you got your act together, you'd have food, utensils, and kitchen stuff at your disposal."

"I have got my act together. It just needs to arrive." Luke huffed, then muttered, "Daisy said the container was delayed coming across."

"Luke," she said with a laugh. "Come on, let's go."

When they reached the sand, Freya slipped off her sandals and carried them between her fingers. Luke was pensive beside her, glancing her way every few minutes. She didn't know what was going through his head. She only ever knew what he thought through his letters. Freya knew his character, but coming back to the island must be hard for him. She had no desire to leave, but he had all the vehemence of not returning. If the rig hadn't shut down, she would still only know him through the written word.

"Penny for them?" Freya asked, coming closer to him as they walked.

He slung his arm around her neck and sighed heavily.

"I don't know what I'm doing. I feel so lost."

"Are you finding it hard transitioning?"

"To island life? Yeah maybe. It wasn't my choice to come home, but I don't regret it. I just think I need to find my purpose."

Freya swapped her shoes to her other hand and wrapped her free arm around his waist. "You'll find your way."

"Let's hope. Look, there's the cove," Luke said and jogged to the opening.

She dropped her shoes outside and crawled through the narrow tunnel to get into the hidden cave. The waves over the years had battered the rocks and made a hole. She didn't think there would be any treasure because she assumed it would take more than four hundred years for a channel big enough for them to crawl through. Once she'd scaled the side of the rock and then crawled the six feet along the tunnel, she poked her head out into the cavernous space with a few inches of water swirling about. They'd never seen more than three inches of water in the cave, which was Luke's theory's premise. He reckoned pirates sent kids through the tunnels to stow away the crates of coins.

Where they all went was anyone's guess.

"There's not much in here, Luke," Freya muttered, looking up twenty feet to the knotty gnarly stone in shiny greys. She jumped down a couple of feet, splashing into the water. The floor was smooth as marble.

"Where does that water come from? We're ten feet up, and yet this cave isn't dry."

"Maybe there was a high tide last night or driving rain."

"It's neither of those two things. Let's go in that direction," Luke said, pointing further into the rock.

They'd been in this cave dozens of times as kids, but nothing ever changed.

"You go on ahead. I'll wait here and have a look around. Maybe I'll scale that wall. There looks to be a load of footholds," Freya said.

"All right, yell if you find anything."

Luke disappeared through another tunnel, his arse shifting away as he crawled through the space. She knew that tunnel to be a few feet long before it opened into another room. It was like someone had built a house but then never finished it.

Grabbing the hard rock lump, she started climbing carefully, testing out each foothold as she ascended. She was close to the ceiling when she discovered a ledge that wasn't visible from the ground. Using her upper body strength, she hauled herself up and sat on the edge with her legs dangling. Puzzled at what had made the ledge, she looked across to the other side and saw another ledge, but again nothing other than rock. Growing bored, she fiddled with the engagement ring, and to her surprise, it came off her finger. She slid it back on and then off like her fingers had magically shrunk after climbing. She toyed with the cave having magical powers or the altitude of her climb. Whatever it was, her fingers were small enough to fit the ring easily.

Freya had given up on it ever coming off. So when Luke told her she could keep it, it didn't matter if it wouldn't come off. Freya tried it on all her fingers and was so carefree, she dropped it onto the cave floor into the shallow water. The diamond blinked and then was gone. Seemingly washed down a hole like there was a plug hole.

"Shit," she said, panic setting in.

She'd had a ring that wasn't hers, and now she'd lost the ring that wasn't hers.

"Luke," she called out.

Clambering down from the ledge, quickly jumping the last six feet, she heard a crack. The ground moved beneath her and fractured like she was on a sheet of ice. The marbled stone gave way, and her with it. She shrieked and threw her arms out to grab hold of the remaining cave floor. There was no purchase as it was so smooth. Acting like a lizard, she hoped she had enough strength in her hands to cling on until Luke could get to her.

"Luke," she cried out.

She was scared she would get sucked down into the water.

Glancing below her body, she saw the ocean with two very old crates dropping the sea bed. The swirling water swayed her legs violently, trying to drag her down.

"What the fuck?" Luke said, then popped his head through the hole in the tunnel.

"It's a fake floor," Freya said shakily as tears sprouted and fell.

A swell of water rushed up and almost tossed her on the flat of the rock beneath Luke but then rushed back down like it was sucking everything in its wake.

"Oh, fucking hell. Hang on to something Freya," Luke yelled, scrambling out of the tunnel and jumping down.

She reached up her arm to grab his hand, but she was sucked under. It seemed so bright, like someone had lit spotlights down on the sea bed. The water was freezing, and she desperately trod water, hoping the surge would send her back into the cave. Instead, the water level dropped again, taking her to the left and under a rock shelf. Freya hit her head on the sharp rocks. She was nearing the end of the breath in her lungs and struggled to feel her way to safety. Then her arm was yanked hard, and she was hauled out of the water and onto the flat in the cave. Hands were all over her as she gasped, heaving her chest to get oxygen into her lungs.

She was terrified to open her eyes and have the reality of nearly drowning confirmed. Warm lips touched hers in a hard kiss, then they were on her temple and forehead. Then she was kissed again, longer but still firm.

Freya opened her eyes to see Luke extremely close. She was sitting on his lap with his arms wrapped around her. He kissed her again, softer, longer and then pulled back.

"You keep kissing me," she croaked through a sore throat.

"I'm just checking you're still alive. You can't die, Freya. I love you. I can't have you die too."

"Luke," she said, cupping his cheek. "I'm okay. I'm alive.

My head hurts, but you saved my life. I'm alive," she reassured him.

He kissed her again, this time so softly she wanted to cry at his tenderness. Small quick kisses on her mouth, pressing as if testing she were real. Then in a split second, the air changed and sizzled, and she wanted a proper Luke Turner kiss. The ones he'd described in her letters. The ones she was insanely jealous of when they were described with another woman. She sighed for a second, kissed him, and kept her mouth against his. His lips moved, his head tilted, and he crushed her chest to his, hungrily kissing her back. Their mouths opened at the same time, and he swiped her tongue for a split second. She moaned at the contact, wrapping her arms around his neck and shifting on his lap to straddle him. He fell back onto the floor, taking her with him and rolling her towards the wall. Legs entwined, he rolled her beneath him. Never in her wildest dreams did Luke feel as good as he did right then. His hips lined up with hers, his hands in her hair, clasping her head for his mouth to devour hers.

"I knew it would be good," he whispered. "I just knew you would feel good, taste sensational."

Luke thrust his hips to hers and dry-humped her for a few seconds. She was throbbing in all the best places as he continued to kiss her. Near death was forgotten. Luke Turner was kissing her like he meant it. Said words that indicated he'd dreamed of this moment as much as she had. Luke liked her, he told her he loved her, and by the hardness pressing against her, he wanted her. When his hand came up and roughly kneaded her breast, she wrenched her mouth away from his and screamed in frustration. Lifting her thighs and pressing her calves to the back of his legs, she canted her hips to get into his rhythm.

"Luke," she bit out.

He was back at her mouth, pulling on her bottom lip with his teeth.

She looked at him, really staring into his eyes. "Luke," she snapped.

Like they were talking telepathically, he sat back on his haunches and tore open the button on her shorts and pulled down the zipper. She lifted her hips and pulled her shorts and panties off. Coming back down to cover her, he roughly pushed down his soaking-wet shorts. She felt his cock at her entrance, the blunt end of him nudging inside and never had she wanted to cry from the sensation more than she did then. The water was lapping at their sides, and a bigger surge added to her wetness every now and then.

"Fucking hell, Luke, hurry," she said, wailing the last word.

"Oh hell no, Peaches, this is going to be slow and steady," he whispered over her lips. "Part your legs wider."

She did as he asked and welcomed his long slow thrust, but as soon as he was fully inside her, it was like he had lost his mind. The quick thrusts came, and so did her orgasm. Ripple after ripple, and her heart beat so hard she feared she'd have a heart attack and really die. Luke carried on fucking her like a man possessed until he came so hard he roared into her throat and stayed deep inside her. Every inch of her was wet, and she didn't know if it was her, him or the sea.

What she did know was that Luke had ruined her for any other man. There was no way she would connect with another man like she had just connected with Luke. And more, she didn't want to even try. She threw her head back to get more oxygen into her lungs as she caught her breath. Her fingers caressed his nape as she counted to twenty. Luke was still inside her, lying half across her putting most of his weight on his hip, which was on the cave floor.

"Luke?"

"I'm never moving from inside you. This is my new favourite place," Luke said with so much conviction she believed him.

"Luke," she said with a sigh.

"I know right? Tell me you feel it."

"I feel it. But—"

"No buts, just another minute," he whispered into her neck.

She continued to stroke the hair on the back of his head and lifted the leg he wasn't covering. The action made Luke sink deeper inside her. Her eyes snapped to his as he tilted his hips in short thrusts. Freya was incredulous that he was still hard after their water-enhanced sex. In a flash, he sat up and had her straddling his legs, still joined. He wasn't looking at her face. Instead, his eyes were trained where his cock was deep inside her getting harder. Freya lifted up an inch and then sank back down.

"Again, do that again, nice and slow," Luke muttered, not taking his eyes off their joining.

His hands clutched onto her waist, and then he lifted Freya. She felt like she wasn't in control of anything, her body, her feelings or her reaction to Luke, her best friend, carefully fucking her. Where the first time was short, brutal and intense, this was loving, measured, and her entire body was heated.

They were still in their tops, and if it wasn't for the fact the cave was cold, she wanted to strip bare and get Luke to play with her boobs. Looking at him, she didn't think she could drag his gaze away from looking at her pussy. He stroked his thumb over the hairs above her clit, and she shivered. Then when his thumb pressed in, she squeezed every muscle in her body. That got Luke's attention.

"I can feel you," he whispered.

"I can feel you too, honey."

He cuffed her neck and brought her down for a kiss. His tongue swept in and out of her mouth at a lazy pace. It seemed as if Luke was set for the rest of the afternoon, but she knew he had to be cold sitting on the ground.

"Luke," she said over his mouth. "I lost the ring."

"I don't give a fuck about the ring."

"But it was worth half of a million," she said, wincing at her words.

"I don't care, Peaches. All I care about is you're alive, and I get to kiss you. That you're letting me kiss you and fuck you. Christ, I've imagined this so many times. I never thought you wanted me."

"I didn't think you wanted me. You were so horrible when you came back."

Luke was still circling and pressing, and Freya was having trouble thinking clearly about what they were talking about. Shudders came down her body and, in turn, his cock.

"Do that again," he said. "I wasn't horrible."

Freya clenched, and Luke dropped his head back and groaned.

"You took one look at the engagement ring and were incredulous that someone had proposed. You even said who the hell proposed to you?"

"Because I wanted to kick the shit out of him for taking you."

Luke clutched onto her waist, pulled her up, and then down harshly until he expanded inside her. She rested her hands on his shoulders and took over, sliding up and down his length, moaning as her orgasm neared its height.

"I'm nearly there," she muttered.

"Just say, and I'm with you," Luke said.

Freya took over where Luke was swirling and brought herself to orgasm while she rocked back and forth. She kept going until Luke came with a shout. He gathered her close, wrapping his arms around her back and his face in her neck. Turning her head, she rested her cheek against his and hummed through her come down. She shifted, but he wouldn't let her go.

"I need to get you off this floor and somewhere warm. You'll get all kinds of illness sitting here," Freya said.

"I thought I was the medic," he mumbled.

"Am I wrong?"

"No. I vote we go back to mine," he said and kissed her mouth.

Then gave her a gorgeous smile that filled her with so much warmth she was having second thoughts about moving.

"There is nothing there," she said.

"There's a bed, Peaches. Plus, if I text Jason, I bet we can raid his freezer for ready-made meals he has personally cooked."

Freya smiled at the thought of not having to cook and eat Jason's food.

"All right, but I need to be home by eight so I can get my school stuff ready for tomorrow."

"That's a deal. Get off me, and we'll see if my legs still work."

Freya laughed and found she imitated a newborn lamb as she stood and staggered around to find her shorts and underwear. Hauling on the wet clothing wasn't pleasant, but her shirt didn't cover enough of her arse to risk walking home in just a top.

She watched as Luke tucked himself back into his shorts and then yanked them into place.

"I might have lost the ring, but I found the florins, or what I assume to be florins," Freya said, pointing to the small pool that had formed in the cave.

They both looked over the gap from a safe distance. The sand hadn't settled enough for them to make out what was in the crates, but the wood with rusted metal strapping was visible on the sea bed twenty feet down.

"A false floor, right? It looked so real the dozens of times we've walked over it. I never would have guessed," Luke said.

"I'm not sure how we'd get to them."

"Me either. We might just leave them to the sea for now. I might give it some thought when I get over the fright of nearly losing you."

He slung his arm around her neck and kissed her mouth, leaving his lips there for a few seconds before he pulled away.

"We just had sex," he muttered over her lips.

"I know," she replied with an eek face.

His eyes were smiling, and then he grew serious. "Was it the fright of nearly dying, or will you want us to do it again?"

"Definitely again, Luke, always if you want."

His smiling eyes were back, and she sighed. Luke's sexy grin was now only for her.

"Let's get back, get dry and get warm. We have a lock to pick."

20

Luke

Freya Riley wanted him. His best fucking friend wanted him. Him, Luke Turner, who didn't have a proper job, who didn't own the house he lived and who had some savings but not enough to leave Copper Island and set up a home somewhere while he found a job.

There were so many things to love about her he didn't know where to start, but when he slid inside her, he thought he was home forever. He didn't know if they'd had sex once or twice because he never left her body between orgasms. Who cared? He wasn't counting as there would be hundreds more to come. She had said forever. He hoped like fuck Freya meant it because he was all in.

He let her into the cottage and then walked immediately to Jason and Heidi's place, hoping they were dressed and downstairs. Luke didn't want to see them getting frisky ever again. Once was enough. Their cottage was in darkness, but he could hear laughter coming from Archer and Erica's place. He jogged down the well-worn path.

"Hey, Luke," Erica said, heaving up from her position on the sofa.

She grabbed her stomach as she stood. "You want a beer?"

"Hey guys, um, no to the beer, I'm not staying," he said, lifting a hand like an awkward teenager.

He thought it was written all over him that he'd had sex with his best friend, but that wasn't possible.

"I can't stay long. I've left Freya up at my cottage. I was after Jason and his freezer," Luke said.

"You did not," Jason shouted.

Heidi jumped next to him and grinned at her husband.

"I don't know what you're talking about," Luke replied. "Can I have your key, please?"

"No, not until you admit it," Jason said.

"Can you narrow it down, so I don't admit something else?" Luke hedged.

"Are you going to marry her?" Jason asked.

"Ohh, Luke, did you and Freya get together? Please say you did and then marry her so she can live next door. I miss my friend being close," Heidi said.

Archer roared with laughter, and Erica looked between all of them, lost.

"All right," he said, raising his palms to them.

"Yes," Heidi whisper shouted.

"Look, something happened. She nearly drowned," Luke said.

All four faces dropped their smiles, and as a group, they came to the wall asking a barrage of questions, mainly if Freya was okay.

"She's fine, but for about two minutes, I thought I'd lost

her. She thought she was going to die, and I think it polarised how we felt about each other, and then things kinda escalated."

"I'm so happy for you," Erica sobbed. "Ignore these," she said, pointing at her tears. "Pregnancy hormones."

"You'd cry at a love story without being pregnant, honey," Archer said.

"True," she sniffed.

"Help yourself, brother and I'm pleased for you," Jason said, handing over his key. "There's plenty of food in the fridge and the freezer. Take some wine. There's a cooler or the wine rack."

"Please get her to move in. I worry about her so far away on her own," Heidi said.

"It's a quarter of a mile away," Luke said.

"Still..."

"You have to pass her house to get to work," he reasoned.

"Still..."

"We're like an hour old. Moving in and marriage is a little way away, don't you think?"

Four heads shook left and right, giving their opinion.

"Fine, whatever. I'm going to make sure she hasn't got any after-effects from falling through a fake floor and probably drinking in five-hundred-year-old sediment."

"What?" Archer said.

"We found the florins but by accident. But more interestingly, we also found a strange tin at the warehouse."

"What's in the tin?" Archer asked.

"Luke won't tell us until he's sorted through it. He's always been the same," Jason said.

"I need to pick the lock first," Luke said. "If I find anything interesting, I'll let you know."

"I want to come and see what's in the tin," Erica said.

"Honey, do you remember the first twelve hours after, you know...?"

Erica cleared her throat and stoked her stomach. "Tell us as soon as you find anything. Should we stop the kids searching the warehouse if there will be stuff belonging to the Turners?"

"Kenny found the tin and didn't tell the others. I'm not sure they're interested in old stuff unless it has batteries. I'll definitely do more walkthroughs when we meet again on Saturday. I love you all, but I need to get back to my girl," Luke said, raising his hand with the key.

"Bye, Luke," Heidi cooed.

Archer and Jason laughed as Erica muttered, "He better not fuck up our plans of getting wed and raising babies together."

Luke chuckled as he walked into Jason's kitchen, grabbed a basket near the laundry room, and filled it up with the makings for a picnic. He hauled his loot out the back, rested it on the wall, ran back to Jason, and tossed him the key. Luke ran away before Heidi or Erica could quiz him further. Lifting the handle of the basket, he went back to Freya.

Putting the food away in the fridge he raced up the stairs to hear the shower on. He stripped his semi-wet clothes, dumped them in the guest bath, and entered the shower stall with her. Seeing the curve of her bottom sway from side to side as she washed her hair was intoxicating. It wobbled in such an alluring way he dropped to his knees and kissed every inch, moving his hands around to her belly. The soap suds made her the perfect kind of slippery. His fingers searched for her centre, but when he couldn't get the angle right from where he was kneeling, he pushed his hand between her thighs from behind and played with her that way. Freya's legs shook as she widened and tilted for him. When he kissed down to the underside of her bottom, she pressed her palms to the tiled wall and dropped her head to watch.

His Peaches was a voyeur.

"Luke, I can't come again, but you feel so good."

"Let's finish washing, and we can get under the covers and get warm."

Luke wanted to fuck her again, but he didn't think he had the reserves either. Their ordeal at the caves was hitting him, and he started to feel the loss of Freya, even with her standing in front of him. She left the shower first after she gave him a sultry kiss.

"Help yourself to a t-shirt," Luke called out.

He heard drawers opening and closing as he washed his hair and then his body. When he towelled off and joined Freya in the bedroom, he found her crossed-legged in a pair of his black boxers and a white t-shirt. Her nipples were hard, poking the material to get his attention. He became hyper-aware of Freya, more than his wet dreams could ever muster.

"Have you broken into it yet?" Luke asked, nodding to the tin in her lap.

"No. Have you got your laptop here? I think my phone is on the seabed. It wasn't on the ground when we left the cave."

"Oh shit. We'll need to get you another one ordered."

"I can do it from your laptop, should get here in a few days."

"Sure, I'll go grab it."

"Can you get snacks too? I think I'm going to crash from shock."

"Are you talking about us?" Luke said, stepping towards her. "Did I hurt you?"

"No," she said, laughing. "I'm talking about holding my breath for so long and thinking I was going to die, and I'd never kissed you."

"Well, we sorted that out," he said and gave her a salacious grin.

"That we did. Now go, snacks and technology."

"Freya," Luke said softly.

When she looked up from the tin, she gave him a wide smile.

"We didn't talk about birth control."

The smile slid right off her face, and then she mouthed *oh shit*.

"No more sex today because I don't have condoms, and I'm not going to my brothers for those. It's bad enough they guessed we'd got together when I went to get provisions."

"They know? How do they know?"

"Jason," Luke said.

"Might've known it was him. He is too astute for his own good."

Freya dropped her head and then brought it up, looking pained. "How did they take it?"

"In no particular order, Heidi wants me to propose and for you to move in before we're married. Erica wants you to have a baby and for me to not fuck this up. Jason and Archer basically agreed with the women. But I should warn you, I might be a little lost now we've crossed a line."

"Do you have any regrets?" Freya asked quietly.

"None. Do you?"

Freya shook her head and then put her hand flat on her belly. "Do you want to marry me?"

"Yeah, Peaches, I want to marry you. But I'm gonna propose properly. You better say yes."

"Let it be a surprise," she said, raising both eyebrows and looking disinterested at the tin.

Luke lunged for her and brought her up on her knees at the edge of the mattress, his thighs pressed against her. He kissed her so deeply she went boneless in his arms.

"You're a cheeky one, Peaches. If you don't say yes, we're still living together and having my babies."

"If you're so set on babies, we won't need condoms, will we?"

Luke couldn't be happier, but he couldn't forget the baggage that came with him. She was happy, relaxed and open to marrying him and raising a family like they'd planned it for years. It seemed too easy.

Leaning back to bring her entire face into focus, he looked deep into her eyes.

"Don't fuck with me, Freya. Are you serious right now?"

"Luke, if you don't want a future with me, then I would seriously consider leaving the island, as I couldn't bear to watch you fall in love and marry another woman. I'm not that strong."

"Maybe you know how I felt when I saw that ring, and you said you had a fiancé."

"No, not even slightly. I'd be devastated. I wouldn't be able to tolerate being in the same room as you. You stayed friends with me. You gotta know I couldn't do that. I'd have to walk away."

Luke gave her a grin. Over the fucking moon, she was into him as much as he was and that the friends line they'd crossed wasn't a mistake.

"It's a moot point, Peaches. What kind of ring do you want?"

"The one at the bottom of the ocean. If you can't get that, then something gorgeous and over the top."

"I'll see what I can rustle up. Now get under the covers because I can feel you shaking, and I don't think it's me this time."

She nodded and stood up next to the bed. She pulled back the covers and slipped under, getting comfortable on his side. She took the tin from the other side and placed it on the bedside table. Luke wasn't sure if she was okay with what happened, but he didn't want to be away from her for too long. It was the middle of the afternoon, but he still went downstairs, locked up, and brought up a basket of food they could nibble on. He put it just inside the bedroom door and saw that Freya was asleep. Luke went back downstairs and grabbed his phone and laptop. Carefully slipping in on the other side of the bed, he propped himself up and opened up his laptop. The screen was already set to the ancestry site, and he was floored to see so many green leaves for a family that didn't have descendants that lived long passed the firstborn.

He clicked through to another web page and searched for the type of tin found in the warehouse, and then when he found the name of it, he searched how to unpick it. He'd wait for Freya to wake up to open it together. Going back to the ancestry leaves, he clicked through the leaves, and his heart stalled when he saw the potential family link.

"That bitch," he hissed quietly, not wanting to wake Freya.

Instead, he messaged his siblings.

Did you know Aunt Cynthia had children?

21

Luke

The emergency meeting was set in Edward Hall's kitchens. Everyone agreed that they needed to process what Luke had learned over food. Jason made them baked omelettes with their favourite fillings. They assembled around the metal table at the far end of the kitchen. Luke brought up the screen for the ancestry site and showed them Cynthia Turner's name and two possible matches to descendants. It also showed a match to the father's name but no indication she had married him.

"She kept that quiet," Archer said.

"I wonder why?" Jason said.

Luke was still so angry he could barely speak, continuing to punch keys. Erica and Heidi didn't have to haul their arses to Edward Hall at six in the morning, so Archer and Jason had left them sleeping. Luke had a mumbled conversation with Freya, who said she wasn't feeling well enough to go to school, so he offered to personally go and see the head teacher to explain why she wasn't coming to work. He had an hour to talk through his game plan with his brothers and then get to school, then he needed to seek out Cynthia and basically ask her what the fuck was happening and then get to his dreaded day job. All in all, Luke thought he had a shitty day ahead of him.

"Has it dawned on either of you what this means?" Luke said.

"She's capable of love after all?" Archer ventured.

"Cynthia Turner, the eldest Turner in her line on the family tree, produced an heir," Luke gritted out. "What we've been doing here is a waste of fucking time."

Jason's eyes widened. "What?"

"He's right," Archer said. "If she had a child and he or she is older than me, then they will be heir to the Turner fortune and Copper Island."

"And that fucking sucks. I don't have a job I trained for, and now I don't have a legacy to work for. I don't even know if I have a future with Freya. For all I know, nearly fucking dying was the only reason she slept with me," Luke grumbled.

"How is Freya doing?" Jason asked.

"She's been chirpier. She doesn't want to go to work, so I'm heading to the school after this."

"What is the name of the father?"

"Jonathan Cranford. There is no record of him ever being on Copper Island. I can't find him on any electoral roll after 1970. This is the only place he pops up. I've applied to get the birth certificates of the two descendants, albeit one of them passed away at birth."

"When was the other child born?" Archer asked.

"It indicates 1983," Luke said.

"That makes them older than me. I was born in 1987. Is there a name?"

"No, I'll need to get the birth certificate first."

"This is huge," Luke burst out. "All of this we're working towards can be taken away in a flash once Cynthia dies and the heir rocks up."

"Don't you think he would be here by now? Don't you think he would be living at Turner Hall?" Archer posed the question like the information wasn't rocking their worlds.

"So many fucking questions. So many fucking secrets," Luke shouted. "I am sick of this whole legacy bullshit. I just want a girl, a house and a job. I want to love all of them and live a simple life. If Cynthia lives as long as Grandfather, I am never going to see that. What is the point of staying on this island?"

Jason and Archer stayed silent as Luke roared through his thoughts. He muttered that he was calm, but somehow, the island had turned him into a jittery wreck.

"Why did Dad have to die?" he said, choking on the words. "Why couldn't I have saved him? We wouldn't be in this mess if I had."

Jason and Archer took a step towards him, but Luke raised his hands.

"I feel like I'm going to lash out, and I don't want that to be with anyone, especially you two. I'm going to clear my head and then get to the school. Freya said as long as I tell Mr Morris by eight, she won't be in trouble."

"All right, brother. You need to talk to either of us. We're here for you. No matter what we're doing. You hear me?" Archer said.

"I hear you, later," Luke said, not looking at either of them.

Archer's words nearly broke him. He'd spewed out his feelings, and his big brother was still there for him.

Taking the buggy to the town, he parked next to Heidi's old house and let himself into Freya's house. He bounded up the stairs and grabbed clothes he thought she would want if she wasn't feeling well. Striding into the school, he ignored anyone looking at him. He was in too foul a mood to indulge in any pleasantries. The head teacher's office was in the same place it had been when he was in school. He'd already spoken with Mr Morris after he found out he was bullying Freya, but he hadn't stepped foot in the office. This time he wanted privacy to share what had happened with Freya.

He knocked on the closed door and then entered when he heard a barked *come in* from Mr Morris.

"What do you want?" Mr Morris said once he'd looked up from his papers.

The bespectacled man looked older than he was. Luke thought he should've retired years ago, but he was still hanging on at seventy for some reason.

"I've come to tell you personally, so nothing gets lost in translation, that Freya Riley won't be in school today."

"Why?" he clipped out.

"She was in an accident yesterday, and I think she's suffering from delayed shock."

"What are you talking about?"

"She nearly drowned yesterday. I had to save her, and it was touch and go for a few moments."

"Likely story," he scoffed.

"What?"

"I said likely story. I bet she's lording it up at Turner Hall, being served breakfast by the servants. Her neatly ironed newspaper ready for her perusal."

There were so many things wrong with what Mr Morris had just said. Luke didn't know where to start.

"She's unwell. I would believe me if I were you."

"You Turners parade around town like you own the place. It's sickening."

"We kinda do, Mr Morris. The Turners own Copper Island, but we never rub people's faces in it. Cynthia rarely comes into the town."

"Is that right? So you think you've never used your power to get your own way like now when you want to spend the day in bed with Freya and faking her illness."

"I'd be very careful about what you say next, Dudley. I'm telling you the truth. I have no reason to lie to you."

"What will you do? Eh? Kick me off the island like your grandfather did with Jonathan Cranford. Exile me so I can never return. Looks like history is repeating itself. Cynthia fell for the wrong man, and it looks like Freya is too. You're rotten, all of you Turners. You make everyone's lives a misery. My life would've turned out differently without Archibald Turner and his sanctimonious preachings."

"What are you talking about? I've been back for two months. What did I do? Why am I getting lumped in with that man?"

"Your aunt fell in love with a teacher, but overnight he disappeared. Most people think he never made it to the mainland, as no one has ever heard from him again. Because Jonathan was ousted for daring to love Cynthia Turner, I had to take on his classes during the day and evening. Work all day, run home to my wife and kids for an hour and then go back to the school until after the kids were in bed. I bet you can guess how much my wife liked that. I did such a great job. They never replaced Jonathan, so I did two jobs for ten years for single pay. By the time I became a head teacher, my wife had gone and taken the kids. Your grandfather thought giving me the head teacher's job was a reward for fixing the problem of one less teacher, but it was too late. I was already alone. So I have no respect for any of you Turners and will never think kindly of any of you. Your aunt is a horror, terrorising everyone who doesn't agree with her, even from her stately seat up on the hill."

Luke was so staggered by everything he'd just heard he wanted to sit down and neck a shot of brandy. Not daring to move in case Mr Morris wasn't finished, he waited to be dismissed.

"I should go," Luke said quietly after a few minutes. "Freya is unwell, and I need to make sure she doesn't suffer from any delayed shock or have a virus from the cave she fell into."

Luke spoke so softly he wondered if Mr Morris had heard. He seemed more slumped than when Luke had first come in. Not waiting for a reply, he heard a strangled sob just as he was closing the door.

Luke walked down the corridor, wondering what kind of damage the Turners had done to the residents of Copper Island and if he would live long enough to right the wrongs. He'd had enough for one day.

Cynthia could wait.

Luke sent a text updating his brothers and headed back to check on Freya.

22

Freya

Luke came back to the cottage and found her curled up in bed, reading on her tablet. She tilted her head up as he walked through the open doorway with a holdall in his hand. One that she recognised as hers.

"Hey, Luke," she said.

Not having spoken since he woke an hour ago, she hadn't realised her throat was so sore.

"I left you a bottle of water on the side," he said, nodding to the bedside table.

She tossed her phone on the carpeted floor and sat up, struggling on the memory foam mattress. The mattress was a foot-high, moulded to her body in such a way she never wanted to leave the bed. Eventually, with the covers tucked under her chin, she grabbed the bottle and twisted it off. She drank half the small bottle and placed it back on the table. Not moving a muscle, she watched as Luke toed off his shoes and put them in his walk-in closet. He came back out shirtless and in cut-off work-out shorts. She watched as he disappeared into the bathroom and heard the shower water hitting the tiles. When he came back out, he had a towel wrapped around his waist. The gulp she took reminded her that she had a sore throat from hell.

"Did you know that's my side?" he asked, his head tilted with a warm grin.

"Should I scoot over to the other side?"

"No, I like you there. Let's get you showered, and then we can get back into bed. I brought clothing, mainly warm stuff, in case we sit out in Archer's back area. Hopefully, you're warm enough in this bedroom."

"I'd be warm enough in my own home," she ventured.

The last thing she wanted to be was a burden.

"I know, but I couldn't monitor you there."

Luke tugged the covers away and then lifted her ankles, so she had to put her feet on the floor. She eyed him curiously as he took her hands and lifted her to standing.

"Arms up, Peaches," he whispered, not looking her in the eye.

She raised her arms above her head, and he pulled her shirt off, leaving her in her panties.

"You're stunning, Freya," he said to her breasts and then lifted his head to look her in the eye.

His searing gaze, full of seriousness and affection, took her aback. "I am not worthy of you, but I'm going to try to be," he said.

Before Freya could reply, he was kneeling, pulling her panties down to her ankles. She stepped out of them, and he took her shirt and underwear in one hand and her wrist in the other. Then, leading her into the bathroom, he pulled off his towel, draped it on the vanity unit and tossed her clothes in the laundry hamper. Then they were under the hot steaming shower.

"Are you okay with using my stuff, or do you want yours?" Luke asked.

Stunned that he thought of her, she immediately answered. "Yours is fine," she said quietly.

Freya didn't want to speak. Luke had never been this attentive, this quiet, this loving. She thought if she spoke too loudly, it would shatter the moment. She took the second sponge he'd hung up for her and lathered her body in suds watching Luke more than she was concentrating on her own hygiene. She washed her hair and then rinsed, getting out of the shower first.

"There's a robe on the back of the door," he said.

He joined her at the vanity unit and helped her with his robe. It fell to her feet and swamped her body. He tied the belt and then tucked his fingers under the lapels, so she was inches from him. She was mesmerised by his eyes searching her face. Was she a closed book because she wanted to tell him everything in her heart but lacked the words?

"How are you feeling?"

"I've been up an hour, and I already want a nap," she said, slumping against his body.

"Let's get you back to bed. I'll bring up some lunch, and we can eat and talk, then I'll let you sleep."

"Don't you have to get to work?"

"Nope, Archer is taking care of things with Jason so I can spend the day with you, make sure you're okay. Don't underestimate nearly drowning has on you. I'm sure you'll feel a lot better by this evening, but I want to make sure."

"All right," Freya said.

She stood on tiptoe and kissed his jaw. "I like you taking care of me."

"And I like taking care of you."

Luke kissed her, taking it deep and wet for a few moments, then backed away, giving her a cheeky grin while he palmed himself. "Get changed if you need your clothes, and get into bed."

Freya didn't move as Luke grabbed a pair of black boxers off the side cabinet and then pulled on a black t-shirt. She couldn't get over how fabulous his body was. She'd never seen him without clothes since they were kids. The tattoos were a surprise.

"I never knew you had body art," she said. "You never mentioned it in your letters."

"It was a phase where I really loved it and then got bored. I don't regret the ones I have but I doubt I'd get any more."

"They're beautiful."

"Stop saying nice words and get into bed."

"Yes, bossy pants."

Weariness swept over Freya as she crawled into bed. He pulled up the covers and then bent to kiss her temple.

"If you're perkier later on, I have a surprise for you, but only if you perk up."

"All right, I'll try my best."

"Peaches, if anything had happened to you…."

"It didn't, Luke. I have a sore throat which is probably from working too many hours at the school. I'm tired, but then that's expected after a shocking experience."

"Okay. I'll go get food, and then remind me to tell you all about Jonathan Cranford," Luke said, walking away.

"Luke," she snapped. "You can't walk away and make me wait."

"Ah, awesome, perkier already. Roll from side to side so you warm up both sides of the bed," he said, disappearing from view.

"No," she shouted.

Freya heard his chuckle and grinned.

"It's not awkward at all having sex with my best friend," she muttered.

Freya ate beef stew and crusty bread and then immediately fell asleep. She wanted to hear how Luke knew who Jonathan Cranford was. She might have knocked her head, but she didn't recognise the name. She didn't hear anything further than Luke telling her he went to the head teacher to call in sick for her.

"Time to wake up, Peaches," Luke cooed into her neck.

She'd been half awake for ten minutes, but with Luke's body pressed against her back while she slept on her side, she didn't want to move anywhere.

"Who is Jonathan Cranford?" she asked.

Luke chuckled and kissed her neck. "Are your eyes open yet?"

"No, doesn't mean my brain isn't switched on. It feels like I'm missing a bit of information."

"That's because you are, and I forgot you were asleep when I found out and weren't at the powwow this morning."

Shifting onto her back and then onto her other side, she opened her eyes to Luke peering down at her. "Hey," she said shyly.

"Hey," he whispered back and pressed his lips to hers.

"This isn't weird, is it?" she asked, praying for a no.

"No, it's like we've always been this close."

"Good."

"While you were sleeping yesterday evening, I stayed

awake and went onto the ancestry website. Dearest Aunt Cynthia had two children."

"Sod off," Freya said and shifted to sitting up cross-legged.

Luke nodded and felt her forehead. "Getting better and better. The surprise might still be on."

"I want the surprise, and I don't even know what it is, but I really want to know about Cynthia's kids."

"The first child was stillborn, and there is no record of much else. The second is alive. Born in 1983, making him or her older than Archer."

"That makes him or her the Turner heir."

Luke snapped his fingers and pointed at her, seemingly impressed. "Exactly. So all of what we're trying to achieve here could be taken away as soon as Cynthia dies."

"Oh, Luke, how do you feel about that?"

"Before the water incident, I was already lost as to what to do with my life, but then you happened, and I was thrilled beyond words you feel the same way about me as I do you."

Freya reached out her hand and cupped his cheek. "But?"

"I still don't have a job I enjoy, and I don't know if investing all our energies into Edward Hall is going to be a waste of time. Cynthia could live as long as Grandfather, and he was a hundred and three when he died."

"Luke, if you decide to leave the island, you've got to know I'm coming with you this time. I'll buy a substantial amount of barely there lingerie to persuade you to stay because Sabrina is the bomb, but I'll follow you anywhere in the world."

"You mean that?"

"With all of my heart. If you're desperately unhappy

staying, even if it's resolved that Edward Hall is safe, I'll move away with you. We're a team now."

"I need to get you a ring, Peaches and book Reverend Sprite," he vowed.

"You need to propose first, honey."

"That too."

He dropped his face out of her view, and all she saw was the top of his head. She leaned in and kissed his crown, and left her lips there.

"Who is Jonathan Cranford?"

She moved back before he lifted his head. Luke grabbed her hips and lifted her onto his lap, then he fell back and brought the covers up.

"All right, story time. I searched through the records and found Cynthia Turner had two descendants, but I don't know any more until I get the birth certificates. It shows Jonathan Cranford as the father. There is no record of them marrying, not under British law, but maybe that was deliberate, so her father never knew. I can't imagine Dad cared, but their father was mean as a snake, and so was their grandfather."

He shifted them to get more comfortable, hitched her leg by the back of her knee, and draped it over him.

"I was already pissed off by this news and had a plan today to go to your boss, tell him you're unwell, then go and see Cynthia and have it out with her. But the conversation I had with Mr Morris was shocking. He knew who Jonathan Cranford was."

"No," Freya said.

"Yes, and he hates him, having never met him. Wanna know why?"

"Yeah."

"Jonathan Cranford was set to be the new maths teacher

at your school, except he was exiled from the island like this is the 1300s. Your now head teacher was only a few years into his teaching career and had to take Jonathan's classes as there wasn't enough time to hire a replacement. He ended up doing it so long, he lost his wife, and she took his kids away to the mainland."

"Holy hell. Who kicked him off the island?"

"My grandfather."

"Why?"

"This is the shocker because he fell in love with Cynthia, and the match wasn't approved."

"Oh no," Freya said. "But she stayed with him, anyway."

"I'm not sure how. She was always at Turner Hall when we were growing up. She hated my mum. They were always fighting. But then I was young when mum left, so maybe that was in my head. Archer and Jason have always maintained the same view."

"I can't imagine anyone liking Cynthia. I know she's your aunt, but she doesn't come across as warm and fuzzy. If your dad was away for three weeks at a time, it would have been the two of them in that big house."

"True."

"So she had two children by him. I wonder where the second child is? What about Jonathan? Is he still alive?"

"There are no death records, so we have to assume he's still alive although it shows he's younger than her, by a few years, four, I think it said."

"I bet back in the 70s, dating a man four years younger would've been scandalous. This island seems to be twenty years behind the rest of the world, making it 1950s mentality."

"Agreed. So we have a few more puzzle pieces, but I think they're from a different puzzle."

"When are you going to confront Cynthia?"

"Tomorrow. I think you're okay with the surprise this evening. It doesn't mean you have to go to work tomorrow if you don't feel up to it. I got the impression that Mr Morris's anger is at the Turners and guilt by association. You got caught up in it. You've covered most of their sick leave. It's about time they covered yours."

"I'll see how I feel in the morning."

"Okay. Are you hungry?"

"Not really, but I might be later."

"Great. Let's go on a little surprise and then we can go to Jason's place for dinner. Everyone is meeting there, and he's cooking."

"Sounds fabulous. What should I wear?"

"Something warm. It's all coming off for the surprise, anyway. But the warm clothing will be good for dinner as they like to eat alfresco, and it may be late Spring, but it can still get chilly."

"You're so sweet when you're looking after me."

"You're worth looking after, Peaches."

He kissed her stupid and then let her roll out of bed to get changed.

They walked across the lawns behind the cottages and past the end. It wasn't long before Freya was led to a secluded area. Large multi-wick candles were lit inside lanterns around a natural steaming pool. The pool itself was lit as well. It looked pretty as a brochure, but her feet were rooted to the spot.

"We're getting back on the horse, Peaches. It's something my dad always said to all of us. Face your fears head-on. This is as much for me as it is for you. Although I think I get the bonus of seeing you wet and naked again."

"Luke," she said, her bottom lip wobbling. "I can't get back in the water."

"I'll help you. This pool isn't deep. I've put underwater lights in there. Heidi came and lit the candles when you were getting changed. I really think we should do this. I know anyone can drown in a puddle, but standing in that water would only come up to your hips."

"Won't it be cold?"

"That's the surprise," he said.

"I thought this secret pool was the surprise."

"Nope."

Luke let go of her hand and went over to a tree. He picked up a set of screens and positioned them around the small pool to give them privacy. He left one of the concertina doors open. Cocooning the pool brought a sudden darkness to the area and, with it, seclusion.

"I'll be with you the entire time. I will not let you go. Come on," Luke said, tugging on her hand.

She let him lead her as she hummed deeply with foreboding until she reached the edge. There was definitely steam coming off the water. The rock edge was not unlike the cave she'd been florin hunting in. The bowl of the pool looked pearlescent.

"All right, as long as you don't leave me alone, not for a minute."

"I promise. I'll get in first and then help you in, but you need to get naked to get the full experience."

"Okay, I trust you."

Luke's face faltered for a second then he grinned wide. He pulled off his clothes and draped them over a rock beside the pool. He then dropped into the water to demonstrate the water only came halfway up his thighs. She pulled down the zipper of her hoodie and put it on top of Luke's clothes. When she saw his nipples harden and he shivered, she hurried with the rest and stood at the pool's side. Luke came right up to her, kissed her midriff, and then wrapped his arms around her legs under her bottom. With one lift, he took her off the ledge and lowered her into the pool.

"You're so strong," she whispered, draping her arms over his shoulders.

"For you," he said. "Put your legs around me."

She lifted her thighs, and Luke put his hands under her bottom, his fingers slipping between her cheeks. Then he carefully sat down and submerged them to their necks.

"You okay?"

"Yeah," she said, clinging on to him for dear life. "It's so warm in here. How did you manage it?"

"It's nature, Peaches. This is a natural mineral spring. The heat is coming from the earth. Pretty cool right?"

"It is. Have you always known about it?"

"I remember Dad saying something about it. But it was Archer's suggestion to bring you here. I thought we could use the pool at Turner Hall, but he said if I wasn't comfortable, then it would be better if only I saw it."

"You have a great brother."

"The other one isn't bad. He has comfort food waiting for you when we get back. It's already ready in the slow cooker, just in case you weren't ready for this. Heidi told me what to pack and got this place ready. Erica wanted to help too, but Archer has forbidden her to walk on uneven ground."

"You have awesome brothers and their wives."

"I'm hoping I'll have an awesome wife soon too."

Before she could reply, Luke lifted her up and then down on his cock until he was fully buried. She let out a long sigh and rested her forehead on his shoulder. It didn't take long before they were softly calling out their climax. Luke beat her to it, but with a little help, she got there too. If ever there was a way to associate water with something good, it would be having sex with Luke in a natural spa.

"I love you, Luke Turner."

"I've always loved you, Freya Riley."

23

Luke

"Bailey," Luke said as he marched into the kitchens at Turner Hall.

"She's expecting you."

"And she thinks I'm coming for a ring?"

"Yes, they're laid out ready for you. You are choosing a ring, Sir?"

"I am. Freya wants something flashy," Luke replied, grinning.

A soft sob came from the stove. Luke turned his head and deflated and then staggered to Maggie, who was wiping her eyes.

"I'm so happy," she said through another sob.

"Are you? You look like Teddy got sick," Luke said.

"I miss that dog. When's he coming back?"

"When Archer is sure he will be safe around the baby, he's not risking anything. If Teddy isn't a good mix, then he'll have to go to another home."

Maggie wailed into her handkerchief and fell against Luke. He'd never seen her so dramatic. A bubble of laughter rose up, and he couldn't suppress it.

"Freya hasn't said yes yet," Luke reminded her as he cuddled her close.

"How can she not say yes?"

"Cynthia Turner. The meddling we're uncovering is beyond anything I could have imagined."

"What did you find out?" Maggie said, suddenly sobering with the news.

"I'd tell you, but if you already know and you are bound by some blood oath, she made you sign not to say a word, I don't want to put you in an awkward position."

"You're a good man, Luke. We appreciate it."

"Right. So let's get this over with. Are you going to be able to cope making a cup of tea?"

"Funny lad, go on with you," Maggie said, smiling through her tears.

Bailey escorted him up the stairs and across the marble foyer. When he got to the morning room door, he paused.

"There are no canes in there, Sir, but can you keep in mind she's eighty?"

Ignoring his first comment, he answered the second. "She lied to us, Bailey. We're here under false pretences, and I will call her out on it. It's the modern way, seeing as she doesn't want us to learn about Turner Hall and Copper Island, it would seem I've discovered why."

"She'll never tell you the whole story," Bailey said.

"That may be so. I think only two people know the truth. Cynthia and Jennifer. Unless I find Jonathan Cranford, then three people know the truth."

Bailey moved his head back an inch as if to take in the name. Recognition crossed his eyes, but Luke meant what he said downstairs. He didn't want to jeopardise Maggie or Bailey's position at Turner Hall.

"Let's go in," Luke said.

Bailey snapped out of his trance, opened the door, and walked in first. "Luke Turner," he said in his deep baritone voice.

Silence greeted them both, but Luke could feel her presence before he cleared the door and looked to the end of the morning room to the conservatory. She wore a navy pair of trousers and a cream roll-neck jumper. Her back was towards them, but Luke could tell she was ramrod straight. She might be eighty, but Luke felt like he was watching a much younger woman spritz her tropical plants.

"I'll leave you alone," Bailey said.

He stepped back and closed the door quietly. Luke strode to the other end of the morning room a few feet away from Cynthia. The ring cases were on display with the lids open. He gave the rows a glance but nothing more. He wanted to take his time choosing a ring for Freya.

"You can choose one. I won't hurry you. While you're choosing, you can tell me about my great niece or nephew."

"You should ask Archer, not me."

"All right. Who are you marrying?"

"The teacher," Luke said, glancing back to the cases.

He had Cynthia in his periphery while he looked at the diamond rings. They weren't as big as the one Jason picked. Moving to the other case where emeralds, sapphires and rubies nestled, he took his time. Cynthia fiddled with her small sapphire ring, so he instantly dismissed getting Freya anything remotely blue.

"You're going to marry a teacher?" she scoffed.

"Now, now, aunty, I wouldn't dismiss marrying a teacher. You like them, don't you remember?"

He said the words like he didn't know how hard they would hit, but he wasn't expecting a direct hit. He tilted his head an inch to see her reaction, relaxing his face, so he didn't show his cards. Each time he scanned right, he had a better view of her.

Cynthia instantly stopped fiddling and was still. So still, he wondered if he'd gone too far. The pain etched over her face was breathtaking. She'd never shown any emotion apart from anger hbefore. Resisting the urge to completely face her and show any concern, he kept scanning. Luke picked out the ring with a large oval ruby surrounded by diamonds. The jewels were set in platinum. It would look stunning on her finger. It was obscenely flashy. If Freya wanted a pretty ring, she could have a pretty ring.

"What are you referring to?"

Luke straightened, picked up the empty black leather ring box with a T in gold script on top, which he assumed was for whichever ring he chose and pushed it into the black velvet cushion. He closed the ring box and pressed the stud clasp to secure it. After slipping the ring into his trousers pocket, he left his hand touching his future. Using his other hand, he raked his fingers through his hair. Could he confront her? Glancing at her fully, Cynthia looked stricken but livid.

"I'm referring to Jonathan Cranford, the almost maths teacher at Copper Island High School."

Cynthia was just livid now. She narrowed her eyes, thinned her lips and breathed in a long lung full of air. If she were a dragon, he wouldn't doubt he would be burned to a crisp as she exhaled through her nose.

"I haven't heard that name in a long time," she said in a whisper. Her body was still unmoving. He expected her to press a hand to her heart, clutching at her neck, and simply lift her hand to strike him.

Nothing but shrewd eyes assessed him.

Luke was pissed off she was playing indifferently. Cynthia had to know there was no hiding now.

"Define a long time?" he said.

He put his other hand in his pockets. Stood feet apart, staring at her, waiting for an answer. Deliberately showing her, he was not leaving until she gave him the answers he needed.

"I don't answer to you."

"You produced two heirs. I know one passed away, and the other is still alive. Jonathan too. With Jonathan fathering the heirs to the Turner fortune, I think I'd like to know why you are now fuzzy about liking teachers. Why do you think my marrying a teacher is below me? Do you believe that to be true, or did someone, say, Grandfather, make you believe marrying a teacher was a scandal. He must be turning in his grave that Archer married an actress and Jason married a nurse."

Luke watched as she reached back and searched for the cane beside her tall, high-backed chair.

Bailey must have missed that cane when he did a sweep. The sight of the head of a lion just before Cynthia curved her thin gnarly fingers around it sent a shiver down his spine.

"You touch me with that cane, and I will burn it and this house. I'll use it as a torch and set light to this horror house," Luke barked out. "Gone are the days where you can punish me with a stick for asking questions."

"Time for you to go," Cynthia said, clutching hard onto the end of the cane.

He personally knew how heavy the lion's head was.

"So you don't deny you sired an heir?" he shouted.

Cynthia said nothing, looking like she'd smelled something foul.

"If you sired an heir, then Archer won't inherit this estate. Again you've given us something that can be taken away when the heir gets here. They're not that much older than Archer. Hell, they'll inherit the whole fucking island. Why aren't they here learning how it's run? Or are they, and that's why you're not teaching Archer?"

More silence followed. The longer she stayed silent, the angrier he became.

"You don't want to impart any knowledge to us. We're not allowed access to anything. We have to find out everything the hard way. I found out you bore an heir the hard way. I found the florins, the hard way."

Cynthia's eyes grew wide at the news of the florins.

Luke was aware he was yelling, but as long as she had her contrite expression, he knew she wouldn't keel over with heart failure. He didn't want her death on his hands.

"Are you going to say anything to what I've said?"

"No," she clipped.

It sounded like a whip lash he felt across his face.

To Luke's surprise, Cynthia left the room first. She walked with the cane her grandfather had used as a weapon with style. He could hear the faint thud as she hammered it to the ground on every other step. Bailey didn't open the door for her. Cynthia swung it open.

Another first.

As soon as she was gone, leaving the door open, Luke turned full circle, not knowing any more than when he came in.

"Sir?" Bailey said from the door.

Luke looked in his direction and clutched the ring firmly in his hand, desperate not to have it taken from him.

"Where did she go?"

"I believe the walled garden. Jennifer is with her," Bailey answered factually but carefully. He searched Luke's face and then scanned his body. No doubt he missed the cane she carried.

"Right," Luke said with a nod, looking around the morning room with his family's portraits adorning the walls, hating they were witness to the downfall of the Turner family.

Bailey snapped him from his thoughts. "Maggie's asking if you want food."

Maggie was a feeder, happiest when she could make sure the people she cared for had full stomachs.

"I don't. I don't think I could manage a bite after my conversation, but if I don't go back downstairs, she'll worry."

"You're good to her," Bailey said, remaining at the open door in his livery uniform.

"She was good to me when mum left, and I was at the mercy of that woman and my grandfather."

Bailey's lips thinned, no doubt at memories of him not being able to help them.

"Let's get you settled in the kitchen. Will Freya be joining us?"

"No, she's gone back to work."

"Archer, Jason and Erica are also in the kitchens," Bailey told him like he needed more persuasion.

Luke smiled. The backup squad were waiting for him.

"Let's go, Bailey."

24

Luke

"And she didn't deny it?" Archer asked as he humped a tea chest from the main door of the warehouse.

Luke opened the lid and saw the packaging inside. He hauled out the straw-like material and carried it over to the recycling bins. They planned to reuse as much of the contents of the warehouse as possible. The packaging would be used to wrap up customers' orders.

"No. She just stood there, looking... I don't know, really. Panicked, pissed off, and a little sad. She is a hard woman to read. She asked me about baby Archer."

"What did you tell her?" Archer asked, bringing over a stack of cardboard.

"That she needs to ask you, not me. She had no answer for that and changed the subject."

"If she wants to know about my life, she needs to come

Lipstick Kiss

and ask me. She knows where I live," Archer replied as they walked back to the entrance of the warehouse.

The kids were throwing banter as they worked. Kenny walked up and down with a clipboard and a spray can sticking out of his long shorts. The cloudless sky made the work hot and sweaty.

"True," Luke conceded, nodding. "I need to get back up to Edward Hall and check in with Jason to see if everything is okay with the wedding today. You got this covered here?"

"Yeah, the kids will be fine with me. Freya's here, and Erica is gushing over the clothes she's found. Kenny is great with the other kids for someone who was at their mercy not so long ago."

"Yeah, remarkable, really. I'm really proud he's worked through it. I'm hoping the other teenagers have an insight that we aren't dripping in money and we do the hard graft ourselves. Hopefully, that will help with Turner PR. To be fair, if Cynthia stays at the house from now on, I think it will help salvage some of our reputations which seem to be in tatters at the moment."

"Do you hear it directly from the townspeople?" Archer asked.

"Not directly, but how we're treated here is so different from Scotland or on the rigs, hell, even when we went abroad. It's bizarre that people will talk to me but not really engage. I swear Mrs Sentry half curtseyed when she saw me in the newsagent the other day."

Archer barked out a laugh at Luke's description and then patted him on the back.

"It will all turn out okay," Archer assured him. "I'll see you later for dinner. Bring Freya."

"See you later," Luke said.

Luke jumped in the buggy and headed for Edward Hall.

When he got to the kitchens, he glanced at Jason and saw a scowl on his face. Then he saw Stan. They were on either side of the metal table in the far corner. The only thing on the table was a spanner. Jason swiped at it, and the tool skidded across the table and clattered onto the floor, skidding again and hitting the skirting board.

Luke suppressed a laugh and went to referee.

"Why are you antagonising the chef, Stan?" Luke said on approach.

"I'm merely the messenger. The bride isn't happy."

"Is it food related?" Jason asked.

Feeling uneasy, he watched Stan pick up the spanner and walk towards Luke.

"It's not, but now another Turner is here and the C&B manager no less. I can pass the spanner onto you," Stan said.

Luke looked to Jason, who now wore a smug grin.

"Not food related, not my problem," Jason said, holding his hands up.

Jason straightened his chef cap and folded his arms like he was in for a treat to watch.

"Is it C&B related?" Luke asked with a sigh, swinging his gaze back to Stan.

Stan was in a navy blazer, blue slacks, a white shirt, and a light blue tie. Luke was impressed. Even though the wedding day running was with the C&B team, Stan came to all the weddings to see them through.

"It's kind of... might be... sorta...." Stan said, giving Luke a multitude of facial expressions. The upside-down smile was worrying.

"I am not taking that spanner from you until I know what the problem is," Luke said.

"She says she bought the dress before she booked the venue, and her mother came here to view the place."

"So?"

"She has a big poofy dress."

"So?"

"Don't you know anything about weddings?" Stan asked, exasperated.

Jason laughed unashamedly.

"Fuck off," Luke said to Jason. "Go bake some muffins. Those dark chocolate ones with melt-in-the-middle white chocolate."

"They're in the pantry. Help yourself. I'm staying for this," Jason said.

It was still early in the day, not even nine. The kitchen staff had started drifting in, chattering as they stored their stuff in lockers. Side glances over to Luke, Stan and the spanner and then smirks rippled about the kitchen team. They all knew what a spanner meant, as some were food-related.

"Stan, what is the actual problem here. Spell it out like I'm a medic and know nothing about weddings. Oh wait, that's what I am."

Jason folded his lips in, and his shoulders shook but remained silent.

"She has a poofy dress, and the wind has picked up."

Luke took one large step back and held up his hands, palms facing Stan.

"I'm not taking that spanner. I cannot change the weather."

"The thing is, when she walks down the aisle, the wind coming in from the west will pick up her skirts, and she's scared she'll have to clutch onto her dress and look like a fool. A bride doesn't want to look awful in the photos as she walks down the aisle with her daddy," Stan explained like Luke was a child.

Several vocal agreements came from the kitchen staff, and much nodding.

"Save me from this madness," Luke muttered. "Give me the spanner and come with me."

Stan gleefully handed over the tool, and Luke tossed it into the nearest bin. "I'll see you for dinner, Jason, at Archer's," Luke called out.

"Wouldn't miss it," Jason called back.

Luke muttered under his breath as he walked out to where they had set up the marquee. The bride was right. The wind had picked up. His t-shirt rippled in the hard breeze as they walked around the tent.

"So the ceremony is this side of the marquee?" Luke asked.

"Yeah, so they get married in the sunlight and not the shade of the marquee."

"Okay, so let's go the other side and see how far away we get from the shade of the marquee, and the wind picks up."

Stan nodded and led the way to the other side. He paced until the breeze flapped at his trousers. "Here," Stan shouted.

"All right. So that's still in the sun. What if we move the platform to this side, set up some windbreakers along the edge of the marquee and move the guests' chairs? Some of them will be in the shade, but I don't think everyone wants to sit in the sun, anyway."

"Sounds like a plan," Stan agreed.

"Let's go talk to the bride. If she agrees, I can grab a couple of the kitchen staff and move the chairs and podium quickly. It's a small wedding, so it shouldn't take long."

Luke sat on the balustrade while Stan walked the bride

and her father down where the aisle would be, pointing out what they would change. When Luke saw both of them nod and a shielded thumbs up from Stan, Luke went to get extra sets of hands.

Once everything was shifted, and the bride gave him a hug from saving her blushes, he jogged back to Sabrina Lodge to get a shower. He didn't expect to find Freya languishing on a living room sofa in the back patio area.

His belongings had arrived.

"Hey," Luke said, bending down and giving her a quick kiss.

"Hey," she said, trying to prolong the kiss, but he wasn't giving in to her. "Why so glum?"

"I can't handle weddings and being a pencil pusher for the business. I've just had to move the entire ceremony set up because the bride decided it was too windy."

"She didn't fancy flashing her knickers, I bet."

"See? I didn't think of that. I am not cut out for this. I don't think on that level. I knew how to solve the problem, but I didn't understand there was a problem until Stan came to me. Well, he went to Jason first, but he stepped away as it wasn't food related."

"Are you really that unhappy?"

Luke looked at Freya and thought about the ring he had stashed away. For too long, he wondered if he would ever give it to her. He needed to be sure he was staying to ask Freya to be his wife. She might have said she'd follow him anywhere, but he would not make her move away from her job and family.

"I am, Peaches, and I don't see a way out. I'm not going to let down Archer, Jason and Daisy but fuck if I know how to solve the problem."

"It'll work out," Freya said, reaching for his hand.

He stepped away. Until he knew for sure he was staying, he could touch her. It wouldn't be fair.

"I need to get a shower, change, and get back to the wedding before it all kicks off."

"Oh, okay. I thought we'd have a bit of time before your duties started."

"Sorry, need to get a shifty on."

Luke saw the disappointment on her face and nearly caved, but he had to be strong. He patted the arm of the sofa and unlocked his back door. Luke was grateful Freya didn't follow. By the time he came back out, she was gone.

The wedding went well. He dashed back to Sabrina Lodge, showered, and changed before searching out Freya.

When he left his place via the front door, he tripped against a giant flower pot filled with earth. There was a note stuck to his front door with the lipstick mark in the corner.

These pots are too big for my place. They'll look better here. Freya.

There was no love, or X. He flipped it over and checked that side, and it was blank. They were the pots he humped from the Lavender farm. She was right. They looked awesome, flanking each side of his front door.

Luke needed to find her.

He called her, sent texts and hammered on her door, but he wasn't getting any answers. Luke even went to the school where Mr Morris had previously said she wasn't working the evening classes, but it was closed up. The warehouse was locked up too. Luke didn't fancy invading best friend code and quiz Heidi about where Freya was hiding out. The same went for her parents' place.

He'd just have to wait it out.

When he got to Jason's place a few hours later, Freya wasn't there.

They finished dinner and were sprawled out on the sofas in Jason and Heidi's living room, watching Archer and Erica bicker over baby names. They were adamant that they didn't want a name on the Turner family tree. Having recently gone through the names in the graveyard, Luke was gleefully clipping out negatives for the names they chose.

"Is there a traditional name that is not on the family tree?" Erica asked.

"There aren't that many on the family tree, to be fair. You could have Owen, Ada, and Stephen. I'm shocked there isn't a Christopher, Isobel, or Maud."

"Maud?" Archer said.

"I had a neighbour called Maud, and she was mean to me. Can't have Maud, but I do like Isobel," Erica said.

Archer nodded at the possibility. "What about a boy? Christopher?"

"Maybe. Let's see when they arrive and decide when we meet them," Erica suggested.

"Excellent idea. Buys us more time. I'm all for that," Archer replied.

"Okay, who wants apple pie?" Erica asked. "I want apple pie, but don't feel you have to have some. Don't feel pressurised at all," she said.

She began getting up, struggling, unable to bend. Archer shifted his hands under her bottom and helped her up.

"I could've done with that at the check-up the other day. No one tells you that you can't do much when you have a big belly when trying to bend. I'm grateful it's warmer. I can wear slip-on shoes," Erica said.

Erica grinned at everyone.

Heidi went to help her in the kitchen, leaving Luke alone with his brothers. Jason looked at Archer, and then Archer looked at Luke.

"What?" Luke said.

"How unhappy are you? With the job, I mean. Although I am slightly concerned, Freya isn't here."

"I seem to have pushed Freya away. I'd forgotten she knows me so well, so when I got distant, she knew."

"Why did you get distant?"

"I don't really know where I fit in. The meeting with Cynthia has really rattled me. Have we got to wait on tenterhooks to see what stunt she's going to pull next? When you came home, Archer, she was clear you needed to get a wife to carry on the Turner name. Now we find out she has an heir. What if he is as calculating as her?"

"I got the lawyers to check over the contract I signed for Edward Hall, and it is all legit. No one can take it away from us, not even Cynthia Turner. So if she can't take it away, whoever is her child can't either," Jason cut in.

"That makes me feel a little better," Luke said.

"I have an idea for a role you might want to consider. It might involve online courses to get a refresher and maybe learn some new stuff."

"I just spent six months learning how to push paper around," Luke said.

He'd learned much more than paperwork but wanted to behave like a sullen teenager.

Archer chuckled, and Jason moved to the edge of his seat, no humour in him at all.

"We think this might be a better fit for you. I have to say you rock the C&B stuff, though. Everyone raves about the service you give for each residential we have here. The brides gush about Stan, but then he's a big romantic."

"Hey, I can be romantic," Luke said.

"You might want to search for those skills when you try to win back Freya," Jason said.

"Okay, what's the idea?"

Archer spoke next, clearing his throat. "I think we could offer mass-event medic training. More crowds were here than I ever remember when the gig racing was on, but there were very few stewards. It's a peaceful competition, but if anyone got into trouble in the water or on land, there weren't many around that were trained to help. If it's down to Daisy and us to get the island busy with tourism, then we'll need to set up more than gig racing. That means more tourists, which means more support staff. We can ask for volunteers, but if they don't know their arse from their elbow or panic in a crisis, it won't help and will have a knock-on effect on tourism. So I thought maybe we could have regular courses at Edward Hall for the events we hold on the island. We could expand and offer the same training to towns on the mainland. It's a huge surfer's paradise, with loads of competitions, which means loads of spectators. They could send their first aiders over here to be trained for mass events."

Luke was overwhelmed by the idea. It sounded perfect for what he'd spent years training for. It was gratifying to know his brothers had faith in his medical abilities.

"I love that idea. Do you think it would bring in revenue?"

"I think in the beginning, the knock-on effect of having more events on the island will help the town get busy again rather than money in the bank. Our other courses and weddings are more than keeping us afloat. But I also thought this would be where you would need some specialised training. You could do one-on-one physio-therapy courses for athletes that have been injured. I'm thinking of ligament damage, and they need to get match fit again. Marathon runners, it could be anyone. But I'm thinking Olympians, those who want seclusion while they get back on their feet and not in the gym where anyone can see them get back to where they once were. You have the medical training, but you'd need to get the physio training. You could do the theory online and then go across to classes. I had a quick look, and it's like a day a fortnight in a classroom environment for practical lessons."

Luke was silent for a long minute and then slumped back on the couch.

"That sounds phenomenal. And you two would support me to do that?"

"If it's what you want, and it makes you want to stay on Copper Island with us, we'd do pretty much anything," Archer said.

"I have the best brothers," I said.

"Daisy did the course research, so she gets kudos too. Plus, she worked out the financials so we could float the idea to you."

"Gotta love practical Daisy," Luke replied.

"I think she knows as well as we do that we're outdoors, practical people and staying cooped up in an office all day won't work. Jason's happy in the kitchens because he still gets to create and feed people. I have the best of both worlds because I get to go around and fix things, and most of those things are outside or in one of the rooms in Edward Hall. I'm not sitting in a chair watching my belly grow."

"No, that's my job," Erica said as she came back into the room.

"Think about it," Archer said to Luke, then gazed at his wife.

"I don't have to. I love the idea. But what about the C&B manager's role?"

"That is a future Turner problem. We can manage the

role between us until the baby arrives," Archer said before kissing Erica's large belly.

"All right, who wants pie?" Erica asked as she pointed the cake slice to all of them. She got four nods, and then Luke nodded to his brothers and grinned.

He had his job sorted. Luke knew he would never get Cynthia sorted, so the only other task was to speak to Freya.

25

Freya

"You're not breaking up with me, Luke Turner!" Freya bellowed as she marched down the quayside as dusk was settling.

She saw Luke leaning against the wall, his arse resting against the stones and his ankles crossed. He turned his head towards her and gave her a dazzling grin. She faltered in her hasty steps and covered tripping up with a hop and a skip. Luke burst out laughing, but when she narrowed her eyes and scowled, he pressed the back of his hand to his mouth and swallowed his laughter.

"Hey, Peaches," he said.

Freya came to a stop a few feet away and put her hands on her hips. She had a letter in her right hand and clutched it firmly.

"Don't you hey me," she said.

"You're the one who has avoided me for a week, not the other way around. You are super stealthy when you don't want to be found. I thought this island was tiny until you disappeared."

"You made it very clear you didn't want me anymore, but I am here to tell you breaking up with me is not on the table. So get it right out of your head."

"It's good you feel that way because I didn't want to break up with you. I wanted you to break up with me."

"What? Why? You are the most exasperating man I have ever known," Freya said.

She turned her back to walk away. She got three steps away, let out a muffled scream, and put her hands on her head. She would never break up with him. She would never end their relationship. It had taken her a week to write the perfect letter to tell him, and then she got a message from Heidi to come to the quayside. Determined to see her speech through, she turned back around.

Then she looked down.

"Oh no, no, no," she said, waggling her finger from side to side. "I'm still mad at you. You can't do this now," Freya said.

Luke was on one knee, holding a black leather ring box open. She thought the ring was stunning and itched to put it on. It seemed larger than the one she lost.

"Freya Riley, I want more than anything for you to be my wife."

"Yes," she said.

"Please let me finish," Luke pleaded quietly.

Luke waited for her confirmation. She nodded and lifted the envelope, and pressed it against her mouth.

"Does that mean the letter will have two lipstick kisses now?" he asked with a nervous laugh.

"Is that it? Is that all you have to say? Can I say yes now?"

"No, Peaches. You have to understand that I love you," he said, then cleared his throat.

"I love you too," she whispered behind the letter.

Luke's face softened, and he smiled his dazzling smile.

"You have to understand that you're going to be marrying a Turner, and one day a quarter of this island and everything on it will be ours. What comes with that is a lot of hate, animosity and history that the Turners should not be proud of. They ruled with a rod of iron and not in a nice way. They bullied, cajoled and dominated what happened on this tiny scrap of land. I opened the tin that was found in the warehouse, Freya."

She gasped and widened her eyes. Luke's face was crestfallen and the saddest she'd ever seen him.

"That part can wait. But you're not just marrying me. You're taking on getting this island dragged into the modern world, and with that comes equality, tolerance, and acceptance. It will be hard work, but I hope I can make you happy that the Mr Morris' of this island won't penetrate too deeply."

"I'll be by your side, Luke, every step of the way. I'll support you and your brothers, their wives, Daisy, and whoever she pulls into the fold. I promise to hold your hand."

"Okay, Freya Riley, will you marry me?" Luke grinned and held the ring box higher.

"Yes," she shouted, throwing her arms in the air.

Somewhere off in the distance, she heard a woman shout yes back. Freya didn't look to see where or who it had come from. She was on her knees in front of Luke, peering down at the colossal ring. She wanted her hands free for the moment he slipped it on, but she still had the letter and no pockets in her dress. Freya looked to her right, saw a loose rock in the quayside wall, and pulled it out. She shoved the letter in and pushed the stone back in place.

"Won't that get damp? I won't be able to read it," Luke said.

"You don't need to read that letter anymore."

"Did you call me bad names in it?"

"Focus, Turner. The ring," she said, dancing on her knees.

Luke took the ring from the box and tossed the box behind him, he slipped the ring on her finger, and it fit perfectly.

"Oh, Luke, it looks gorgeous and expensive."

"It is. I'd be grateful if you could try not to lose this one. I don't want to return to Cynthia if I can help it."

"You need to kiss me now," she whispered.

Luke took her by surprise by wrapping an arm around her back and lifting her bridal style. He stood still for a moment and stared at her like he couldn't believe she was there.

"I'm not going anywhere, Luke," she said, stroking his cheek.

"Okay," he replied and then kissed her deeply.

Then he carried her to the buggy waiting for them at the end of the quayside. He placed her on the front bench seat and then returned to get the ring box. Once he was settled, he turned on the ignition.

"Let's go to Sabrina, and you can judge where I've put all the furniture."

"Luke?"

"Right next to you," he replied as he drove them up the path.

"I want a big wedding," she said.

"I know a wedding planner who can help," he said, giving her a side look.

"I want to get married at Edward Hall."

"The wedding planner is exclusive to Edward Hall, Peaches."

"I know what dress I want," she said.

"Erica will make your bridal dreams come true if you need a top designer."

"I have a folder, Luke. I know exactly what I want."

Luke pulled the buggy over to the side under a canopy of trees. He turned off the engine and shifted away from the steering wheel while at the same time hauling her over his lap, so she straddled him.

"Freya?"

"Yeah? I'm right here, sitting on your erection."

"Babe," he said and hissed when she ground against him.

"Honey," she replied.

"You take that folder to Stan. You take Erica and Heidi with you. If you wait until Daisy is back, take her too. Have whatever the fuck you want for the wedding day. It will be a small price to pay for dragging you into Turner history. Are we clear?"

"Yeah, the thing is, I have two folders."

"Okay?"

"One where my dad was paying, and you wouldn't be my husband. Then the other where you were going to be my husband."

"What am I missing here?"

"Is there a budget?"

"Fuck no, have what you want. I'll steal a few more rings if I have to. Or go diving for the florins."

"Okay," Freya said.

"Why are we having this conversation?"

"Because Archer and Jason got married quickly and quietly. There was barely any time to get Heidi ready, but I want the whole thing, the whole experience. I want my mum to be the mother of the bride and wear a fancy hat. It sounds so superficial, but I've wanted to marry you for so long."

"Now I want to marry you tomorrow," Luke said. "Not to cheat you out of a wedding, but because I think I fell a little bit more in love with you."

Freya sagged against him at his words.

"You'll need to wait, and we're abstaining," Freya said.

"The fuck we are. You can have the wedding of your scrapbook dreams, but I am not giving up worshipping this body."

To show he meant it, he slipped his hand under the hem of her dress and found the edge of her panties. He pushed them to the side and slipped his fingers inside her. When his thumb joined, she was moaning and clutching at his shoulders.

"You want to give this up?"

"No, I was joking, I promise."

"Ride my fingers, Peaches. Show me how much you love it."

Freya was already wet from his proposal. It didn't take her long to get her orgasm and for Luke to drive like crazy back to Sabrina Lodge to strip her bare.

26

Freya

"Your forearm is really bumpy," Freya said, trailing her fingers along his arm.

"Yeah."

"Is that why you had the tattoos done?"

Freya didn't give him time to answer. She sat up in bed, letting the covers drop to her waist. Luke was still half asleep. Her eyes flicked to his face to see him lazily staring at her bare breasts. When she started to move, spreading her fingers over his chest, he shoved his hand behind his head with his elbow bent. The other hand that was nearest to her body cupped her breast to feel its weight.

"Stop distracting me," Freya huffed.

"You're feeling me up, so it's only fair I get to do the same."

Freya paused for a second, considering his point. Then, deciding it was valid, she continued her exploration but didn't get far. She found herself on her back, pressed into the mattress, when Luke covered her body with his.

"Are you sure you're okay with no protection," he asked gently as he slid inside her.

Freya wasn't concentrating on his question. Instead, she was tilting her hips just so as to get the best friction from his gentle thrusts. His head loomed above her, his fists on the mattress. She stroked her hands up his biceps and then over his shoulders until her fingers threaded into his hair. Freya closed her eyes and eventually answered him, raising her knees to her chest and brushing against his ribs.

"If you get me pregnant, I have a ring on my finger that says you want forever with me. I don't care if I'm in a maternity wedding dress walking down the aisle. I want you, Luke Turner, however, that happens."

"Christ," Luke whispered and moved faster.

Their sighs and moans were quiet as they fucked themselves into oblivion.

Freya took his weight for half a minute and then rolled out of bed to get cleaned up. Luke joined her in the bathroom, shaving while she showered.

"Why are you shaving? It's Sunday?" Freya asked as she wiped away the steam from the shower screen.

His hand stopped halfway up his cheek, leaving a clean sweep in the foam. "We're going to Sunday lunch with your family," he said.

"It's at Heidi's family home. You've been there before. You've met them a hundred million times."

"But it's different now," he said, going back to his shaving. "You have my ring on your finger. I'm going to do things right."

Oh no.

"Oh no. No, Luke Turner. No, no. And no again."

"Yes, Freya Riley. Oh, yes. Yes, and another yes to add to the stack of yeses."

"But there is no need," she wailed.

"Get your arse out here," Luke said, wiping off the excess shaving foam.

If she wasn't so mad and apprehensive, she would melt at his panty-dropping grin.

"I'm going to take your father to one side and ask permission to marry you. I don't care that I've known him since I was five," Luke said.

"But he'll think you're a pompous arse."

"He won't, and I'll tell you why. You are his only child, and you are a daughter. I don't care how much the modern world has accepted gender equality. You are his to protect. Your dad and your mother think the sun rises and sets with you. I'm going to seek his permission."

"Luke," she said, sniffing.

"Peaches," he said through a laugh as she hugged him.

She never thought she'd be comfortable with naked hugs, but naked hugs with Luke were the best.

"You're worth it, Freya."

"I love you, Luke."

"I love you too, Freya. Now get dressed. I'm doing this, but it doesn't mean I'm not shitting my pants because I don't have a plan if he says no."

Freya leaned her upper body back, and Luke's eyes immediately went to her breasts squashed against his chest. She felt him against her pelvis and grinned.

"Now, get out of my sight, so he doesn't get excited and think we're spending the whole day in bed."

Freya swayed against his growing erection and then exited the bathroom. Not fast enough because she got a swot on her backside for cheekiness.

They arrived at Heidi's family home and were greeted by Heidi's mum. Freya's mum soon rushed to the front door and hugged Freya like she hadn't seen her in months.

"I saw you a few days ago. What's with the bear hug?" Freya asked her mum.

"I saw you for ten minutes three days ago and hadn't seen you for a week. You work too much."

"Not by choice, Mum. Fingers crossed, the next head teacher is a little fairer with an equal distribution of extracurricular activities."

"No guarantees with Cynthia heading up the board of governors," Freya's mum muttered. "Oh, I'm sorry, Luke. I didn't mean that."

"That's okay, Mrs Riley. We all feel the same way."

Freya's mum gasped and then giggled. "Come in, you two. The roasties are hidden, so don't go looking for them."

"They're in the oven. That's not hidden," Freya said.

"Well, I've hidden the oven gloves."

"Like that will stop me, but I'll be on my best behaviour seeing as Luke is here."

"Is Mr Riley in the TV room?" Luke asked.

Freya jumped out of her skin when her mum clamped her palm over her mouth and screamed full-on. It was muffled, but it startled Freya.

"Mum, calm the hell down."

"I will not, Freya Riley. Let your mum be excited. Have you dusted off the folder?"

"My house is not dusty," Freya said, put out at the accusation.

"Are you lot going to stand out here all afternoon?" Heidi said, coming back to see why they hadn't entered the house. Heidi's mum soon followed to see what the delay was.

"Luke wants to see Freya's dad," Freya's mum announced.

"Christ," Luke muttered.

"Don't you be getting exasperated. It was your idea," Freya said, jabbing her finger into his chest.

"Oh, I wondered why you were in a shirt," Heidi said, nodding. "Nice touch."

"Let's get this over with. If he says no, then it's all on you, and the folder will go in the incinerator," Luke clipped out, pushing through the women to get into the house.

Freya gasped at his comment. She wanted to dash home and put it in a fireproof safe.

"Can I see the ring?" Heidi said.

Freya thrust her hand out.

"Wow," Heidi said. "Like wow, you cannot lose that one. Wow."

"I know where the other one is, so technically, I didn't lose that one. I just don't fancy diving into a whirlpool to get it."

"I'd rather you didn't either, Sweetie," her mum said.

Luke came rushing out of the house and glared at Freya.

"What did I do?" Freya asked.

"I got three words out, and he said yes. Not even the whole sentence."

"Like father like daughter. That's a good thing, right?"

"I suppose," Luke said, grabbing her hand. "Come on, Keith said we're allowed a celebratory roastie before lunch."

"Yay," Freya said and was gleefully dragged into the house and to the kitchen.

All the men were hip to the kitchen island, sipping beers and arguing over nothing. They silenced as soon as Freya came into the room.

"What are you lot gossiping about?"

"Nothing much, honey," her dad said. "Let's have a look at the ring then."

Freya stuck out her hand and then slowly lowered it to the bowl on the counter with roasties in. She clutched the potato like she was playing an arcade game, grabbing a teddy, and lifted her hand.

Jason whistled when he saw the ring. "You chose a whopper," he said to Luke. "At least I chose from the bottom row when I went for the diamond."

Freya looked at Luke, and he was already looking at her smiling. "I chose what you asked for," he said, shrugging.

"Which row?"

"Top row, Peaches."

"Yes," Freya hissed with a fist punch in the air.

"That's my inheritance you're wearing, so you need to be careful," Luke said.

"How much of your inheritance?" Keith queried, joining the group.

"I'm not sure I should say," Luke hedged.

Jason piped up. "Freya, do you remember the value of the other ring?"

"Yeah."

"Well, that's worth ten times more."

"Luke," Freya said.

She dropped the hot roast potato on the floor and staggered back a step.

"Bloody hell, she let go of a roastie. She must be truly shocked," Freya's dad muttered over his beer bottle.

"What? You asked for flashy. I got you flashy. Wait until you get the eternity ring. That's when our first child comes, right?" Luke said.

A beer bottle slammed down onto the counter.

"Calm down, dear," Freya's mum said to Freya's dad.

"Freya?" she asked gently.

"I'm not pregnant, Mum. Relax."

She was still staring at Luke.

"I better text Archer the rules of an engagement ring," Jason muttered, ignoring Freya's dad's shift in mood.

"Freya," her dad's voice boomed out.

"Honestly, Dad, I am not pregnant."

"Okay, honey, but I know how to use a calendar," he replied. "You got engaged before permission was granted. We don't want everything else backwards."

There was a smattering of giggles at Freya's dad's comment.

Freya snapped out of her shock and stepped towards Luke. "You got me a top-row ring?"

"Yeah, you still like it?"

"I love it, I do."

"Well then, stop worrying about the cost and admire the beauty. I know I am," Luke said.

That got a sigh from the mothers and grumbles from the men.

"It's insured like the other one was. So please don't worry about the value."

"Okay," she said. "I love you, Luke Turner."

"I love you too, Peaches. Now, let's have some food before I keel over from the stress of asking for your hand in marriage."

Everyone got busy with their tasks as they had done on so many Sundays before and were soon seated around the table.

27

Luke

Luke had fallen onto his back on the outdoor sofa and taken Freya down with him when they returned from Sunday lunch. They hadn't reached inside before they collapsed from carb overload. Luke had moved Freya, so her back was to the back sofa cushions tucked into his side. He'd hauled her leg up by hooking his fingers behind her knee to drape it over his thighs. Lastly, he positioned her palm over his heart and put his hand on top.

"Comfy?" Freya asked sleepily as she burrowed in further.

He fiddled with her engagement ring before he answered. "Yeah, this is perfect for an afternoon snooze."

"Do you think the others are doing the same?"

"More than likely."

"But obviously not Archer and Erica if we're lounging on their sofa."

"This is mine. Archer got fed up humping the stuff I

always took from their place. Each cottage has the same furniture but in a different colour. I stripped the house and took it all to the storage rooms at Edward Hall. Looks like Archer decided I liked Turner furniture after all my bitching about wanting none of it in my home."

"It's very comfy. I approve," Freya said.

She rested her cheek on his shoulder, and Luke turned his head to kiss her forehead. He never wanted to move.

Luke knew he couldn't fix his relationship with his aunt. They were too far apart in morals for that. She'd done too much damage to him for that connection to be repairable. His brothers and sister had grouped together to give him a job that made him happy. And now Freya had his ring on her finger. It was enough.

Finally, he had enough in his life to make him happy.

"When are you moving in?" he whispered into her hair, holding her tight.

"After the wedding?" she muttered.

He didn't take the bait because he could feel her cheek bunch up and knew she was smiling.

Freya was silent for a few moments, so he pitched his idea.

"I was thinking as soon as school breaks up for the summer holidays. Then if Mr Morris makes you work long hours in the next few weeks, I can be gallant and come and pick you up and drive you home. Then fingers crossed, you'll be pregnant by the time school starts, and I can be overbearing and escort you home and take you to work."

"Luke," she said and sighed. "Don't make Dad get his calendar off the kitchen wall and count the weeks."

"That was so funny. I bet he's not really outraged. We're going to give him his first grandchild, hopefully, the first of many."

Freya giggled against his chest. She lifted up her hand to angle her engagement ring. Luke threaded his fingers through hers and brought it back down to his chest.

"Is it really worth six million?"

"Roughly."

"The Tuners are seriously wealthy."

"Technically, Cynthia is wealthy. As we're not allowed to see the bank accounts, I would say the Turners are asset-rich rather than cash-rich."

"How does Cynthia earn an income?"

"I'm not sure. The lease rentals on the properties on the island would keep Turner Hall warm and lit, but that would be it. And maybe only her wing. We've all wondered about the money that comes from keeping this estate pristine. I know the Turner Corporation has businesses overseas, but which ones will remain a mystery until Archer inherits. Then all the secrets will—"

"Luke Turner," a woman yelled.

For a moment, Luke thought it was Cynthia hollering out his name. Then he realised it was Jennifer. He stilled on the sofa and felt Freya do the same. They stayed entwined, their fingers clutched together, waiting for more.

Luke wondered if it was Jennifer.

"Luke Turner, come out of that cottage right this minute," Jennifer yelled.

For an eighty-something woman, she had a loud commanding voice.

"Who is that?" Freya asked, lifting her body up on a straightened elbow, her hand deep in the cushions under his torso.

Luke didn't want Freya anywhere near Jennifer, more so if Jennifer was angry.

"That's Cynthia's handmaid, Jennifer. Christ knows why

she sounds so angry. She never comes to these cottages. If Cynthia was dead, they'd send Bailey to see Archer."

Freya looked at him, stricken.

"That sounds so cold."

"If she was a nicer woman, we would be at her bedside and know if she was unwell. The sad fact is, she is a cruel person, and the staff will follow protocol should the head of the Turner family pass away."

"That makes me sad."

"It won't be the case with our generation. We are going to be a loving family, sharing each other's lives. Support through the downs, celebrate the ups and improve Copper Island."

"I'm looking forward to it."

"Stay here. I'll go and see what she wants."

Luke sighed heavily, reluctantly unentwined his legs and arms from Freya and swung his feet to the ground to slip into his trainers. He didn't bother lacing them up and stuffed the ends into the sides of his feet into the trainers. Luke hoped the conversation wouldn't take long.

"You need backup. Just yell my name," Freya said.

He loved her for that, wanted to hug her, and never let go.

Jennifer had stopped fifty feet from Jason's cottage, clearly not knowing who lived in which cottage. Luke assumed she knew the first three were occupied as she looked at each one in turn. As Luke stepped onto the grass, he glanced down the row to see Jason and Archer sitting on their low walls, arms crossed, knees apart, and feet planted.

To anyone else, Jason looked relaxed, but Luke knew he was anything but calm on the inside. While Jason was barefoot, Archer had his trainers on. Big brother was ready to come and assist if needed, even if it was against a woman in her eighties.

When Jennifer clocked Luke striding across the grass, she moved a lot slower towards him, clearly struggling with a hip or knee problem. He assumed she started bellowing after she couldn't manage to walk any further. It wasn't a quick walk from Turner Hall and would've taken her twenty minutes.

She leaned heavily on a cane. Something that sent a shiver up his spine.

The first thing he thought was, did she need the cane? Was she faking being frail? It was an unkind thought, but he remembered Jennifer from his childhood.

"What did you say?" she shouted when he was close enough.

"To whom?" Luke asked, ensuring he got his grammar correct in front of this woman who was a stickler for correctness in every form.

Sometimes he thought Jennifer was more like the old-generation Turners that his grandfather was.

"Don't get smart with me, boy," she hissed.

Archer and Jason's cottages were to his left, Edward Hall was in the far distance behind Jennifer and somewhere behind him were Freya's loving arms.

Archer had stepped onto the grass a few feet in front of his cottage. Erica was now standing in his periphery, her hand on her swollen belly. Jason stood next to Archer with his hands in his shorts pockets. He was wearing trainers now. Movement caught his eye as Freya wandered to Heidi, and they walked to where Erica was leaning against the wooden post of their back patio area.

"I only want to speak to him. You lot can go back inside," Jennifer shouted to them.

No one moved.

The air was so still Luke could've sworn the tree branches were holding their breath.

"Will you say what you've got to say, Jennifer? I've had the best day celebrating my engagement. Don't kill my buzz."

"The doctor is with Cyn," Jennifer said.

Luke tilted his head, not caring much about the news.

"You mean Miss Turner, right?"

"Yes," she clipped. "Miss Turner," she corrected, getting red in the face.

"Okay. She's eighty. I'd be surprised if the doctor wasn't with her weekly."

"She collapsed."

Her words came out as a wail, seemingly trying to get him to be as concerned as she was.

"What has that got to do with me?"

"You caused her heart attack," she shouted.

"She's had a heart attack?"

Luke switched to a medic in a moment. Jason and Archer were on the move getting closer but stopped five feet away.

"She thinks she did. She had pains in her chest."

Her voice had lowered in volume but not lessened in pain.

Luke remembered for a moment that this woman had been at Cynthia's side for sixty years. Luke's mind took a stand-down approach. Pains in the chest could mean anything. It could be heartburn from her Sunday roast.

"When did this happen?" Luke asked, getting to the bottom of the link Jennifer was making between his conversation with his aunt and her situation right then.

"Two hours ago, I waited until you returned," Jennifer said.

Luke instantly looked to Turner Hall. He could just about see the roof. Had she camped out in the attic rooms to wait for their return?

"How is she now?" Luke asked.

"Like you care," she snarled.

"I don't care. I hate her. But I don't wish her dead."

Jennifer narrowed her eyes, leaning forward from the waist.

"Where's the tin?" she asked quietly.

Is that all she cared about?

"Fuck the tin. Is my aunt okay?"

"Luke Turner," she snapped.

Luke let out a strangled groan, looking to the skies for help.

"You're as bad as her for asking questions to which you already know the answer. You know what I said to her because she told you. You also know I said those words a few days ago. So if she is suffering from angina, clogged arteries or a heart attack, that's on her. That's her guilty conscience plaguing her."

"Her conscience is clean," Jennifer shouted.

"The fuck it is. I remember it differently. I remember what you did too. How's your conscience these days? How do you sleep at night?" he sneered.

Jennifer didn't answer. She huffed and moved her mouth around like she was chewing a lemon. Luke knew she didn't have a clean conscience.

"If she dies, it will be on you. Just like your dad's death is on you," Jennifer barked out.

"Jennifer, that's enough," Archer said, coming to stand next to Luke.

Jason flanked him on the other side.

Jennifer looked at each of us in turn, her mood sourer as the seconds ticked by. Luke couldn't believe she had the balls to call him out on his dad's death. It's a line his aunt had used often. Why did Jennifer care? She was the hired help. He couldn't see her in the same light as Maggie and Bailey. They had both taken care of him when he needed it and sometimes when he didn't. He could make his own breakfast, but he found something about sitting in Turner Hall kitchens comforting. With his brothers standing next to him and his soon-to-be wife behind him, the strength they gave him straightened his spine and filled him with courage.

"I didn't kill my dad, Jennifer. This place did. If anyone is to blame, it's Cynthia and her selfishness. Do you remember the last time I told her she was selfish? Do you? The day I accused her of getting rid of my mother?" Luke bellowed.

Luke knew the moment Jennifer remembered what he was talking about. She took a step back and tightened the belt on her long bottle green cardigan, resting the cane against her hip. She was no longer as feeble as she first made out.

Clearing her throat, she said, "I do what she says."

Luke was shocked she could twist what happened and excuse herself from any blame. It begged the question, what did Cynthia have on her. Or, what did Jennifer have on Cynthia that she had the audacity to call out Luke on perceived bullying.

He was done with this woman and the secret he'd buried so deep it had begun to fester. It wasn't until the split second that he thought he would lose Freya to the water that he knew. Luke knew it wasn't watching his father die in front of him that caused him pain. It was the incident in the library.

The shame ate away at him.

"You watched her beat me with her cane," Luke yelled. "You guarded the door when she struck me over and over again." Luke drew a breath, trying to keep his temperament even. "I was a child."

Archer and Jason both looked at him, but Luke was so angry, hurt, and in pain, at the memory, he couldn't look at them. Slowly he unbuttoned his shirt. Once the last one was undone, he shrugged it off and let it drop to the floor.

Jennifer paled, trying not to look at his torso, yet Luke watched as her eyes went to the area.

"Do you like my tattoos?" he barked out. "Do you notice they're only on one side of my body? The side of my body that was at the mercy of her beating? When I was curled up on the floor, holding my arm up to take the blows. Do you remember the sharp edge of the bottom of the cane scratched down my side, ripping my shirt?"

Jennifer's eyes welled up, but Luke didn't care if she had feelings about that day.

"Do you?" Luke shouted.

"You should go," Jason said to Jennifer.

Luke ignored Jason speaking and stepped closer to Jennifer, lowering his voice.

"You guarded that door while Daisy was hammering on it, bawling her eyes out while I was screaming at Cynthia to stop. You allowed that to happen. Dad was on the rigs, Mum had gone, and Jason and Archer were at school. I dared to ask her why she didn't try to convince mum to stay. I told her she was selfish. I got beaten for it. I was a child unaware of the levity of what I was saying. Looking back, I can see it may have been rude to ask or mean to comment. Do you think I should've been beaten?"

"I'm sorry," Jennifer whispered. "You've got to understand—"

"I have to understand nothing. I was nine," Luke hissed. "Nine years old and having no idea what I was asking apart from being heartbroken my mum didn't love us enough to stay."

"Luke, that's not what happened," Jennifer said.

Luke watched as her expression changed from compassion to guilt to something completely foreign to him. He didn't know what to make of her pale face and shaking hand. Jennifer lifted her cane, and Luke immediately felt sick and stepped back. Jason and Archer stepped in front of him.

"I wasn't going to hurt you," Jennifer said, her eyes welling up again.

Luke didn't answer her. He swiped up his t-shirt and bunched it up in his hand. Then thinking better of it, he tossed it aside.

"You should go Jennifer. You just told Luke that Cynthia may have had a heart attack. He's a medic. Our Dad died of a heart attack. He died in front of Luke's eyes, dead before he hit the floor. What you just did was cruel. And I swear to god if her suspected heart attack was heartburn..."

Luke didn't hear any more Archer said as he strode across the lawn towards Sabrina lodge. He didn't look in Freya's direction, who was still standing next to Erica, and he held out his hand. He heard her run full pelt towards him, and as soon as she was in reaching distance, he swept her up into his arms and carried her the rest of the way to his home.

"I love you," Freya whispered against his cheek as she pressed her mouth to his skin.

"I don't think I would've been brave enough to admit I was beaten if I didn't know you'd be here to hold me."

"Luke," she sniffed.

"Don't cry, Peaches. I'm just about holding on here. Let me get inside the house."

"Okay," she said. "Okay."

She held onto his neck with both arms and pressed her mouth against his neck until they were in his bedroom. She undressed him as soon as her feet touched the floor because he was shaking too much to undo his trousers button. Then she removed her clothes. Luke pulled back the covers for her to slide under, and he joined her there. A moment or two later, he was inside her. Not moving. Covering her body with his. She took his weight as they sank into the memory foam mattress. When she wrapped her legs around his waist and her arms around his neck, he let out a sob he felt come from his toes. All the grief he felt for his dad came out, his sorrow for not having his mum around to console him. Every bone in his body ached like he'd run a marathon.

Freya was there, wrapping him in a cocoon and keeping him safe.

"I love you more than you can possibly imagine, Freya Riley," he said.

28

Daisy

She hadn't remembered that day hammering on the study door until Luke had just yelled it at Jennifer. That was the day she'd had to stay home because the junior school she and Luke attended was flooded. The high school wasn't affected, and Jason and Archer had to go to school.

Luke and Daisy were skidding around the foyer when Cynthia called him into the study. He was taking too long, and she'd grown bored waiting. Daisy was just about to knock on the door when she heard her brother scream out and then heard something whack against something and then another scream.

She didn't know why she hadn't said anything. It was like she'd been brainwashed to forget until she watched the scene play out a month ago.

She'd never felt more lonely with her brothers now married or engaged. With no friends on the island, she was at a loss for what to do. That was why she'd slipped away that day a month ago when Luke had an argument with Jennifer. She still had her bag packed from arriving. She snuck away, boarded the ferry she'd arrived on, and sailed back to the mainland. She travelled by train and then by plane to a hotel in the Pacific and drank cocktails.

But now she was back and had chosen the worst weather to fly in. When she'd left the mainland, it was a cloudy afternoon with light rain. When the helicopter landed with twenty terrified-looking passengers and her gripping the nearest object, it was nasty.

It was the kind of summer storm she'd seen many times while living on the island as a teenager. Driving rain, fierce winds and the waves crashing against the rocks. Climbing out of the helicopter, she grabbed her case on wheels and ran across the tarmac to the cover of the terminal building. It had seen better days, but it was dry.

Her brothers knew she was flying in and which flight, so when she came out of the front of the one-storey white building, she was disappointed to find no one waiting for her. No sign of Heidi, Erica or Freya either. Not that she expected Erica. She was near her due date and had elected to stay at Emma Lodge, their cottage, for the last couple of weeks. Apart from Saturdays, she was setting up for her charity when she went to the warehouse. Daisy didn't know if she was at home or the warehouse as it was a Saturday. It wasn't far. She could make a run for it there and catch a lift up in one of the buggies.

Daisy waited in an alcove sheltering from the storm, clutching at her skirts and attempting to keep her hair in a ponytail, using her hand for a band. After five minutes, she checked her phone. In the family messaging group, there was a message all in capitals.

Luke: SOS, WAREHOUSE, ALL THOSE WHO CAN GET HER SAFELY, GET HERE. ERICA IS IN LABOUR.

"Shit," Daisy muttered as she tucked her phone away in her cross-body cloth bag.

Grabbing the handle of her case on wheels, she started at a jog and then moved into a run. The warehouse wasn't far from the airstrip. By the time she arrived at the warehouse, she was soaked through to the bone. It was the middle of the day, but the dark storm clouds made it feel like four o'clock in mid-December. Daisy hurried along the quayside where the warehouses were situated. They were all closed up, no doubt, because no one in their right mind would be out in a storm like this.

Except her.

Daisy was out of breath by the time she reached the door to Erica's warehouse. It was wide open, banging in the wind. All the lights were on, but she couldn't see anyone. Then she heard a baby's wail. She immediately burst into tears, not that anyone would notice because her face was soaking wet from the rain.

Daisy closed the door but left it unlocked. Leaving her case, she followed the baby's cries. A group of exhausted people was at the other end of the vast room behind a stack of tea chests. Kenny was slumped against the brick wall cradling a baby in a blanket, muttering and smiling at the tiny little baby. On the adjacent wall were five teenagers, round-eyed and looking terrified. They looked up when they saw Daisy approaching the corner and scrambled to their feet. Daisy stepped forward, and they pointed to her right. She turned her head to see Archer cuddling Erica against boxes and Luke sprawled out on the floor on his back with a stupid grin on his face. They looked like they had been through hell and back. Except for Kenny, he looked happy holding the baby. Kenny stood deftly and came to crouch beside Erica.

Luke looked at what was happening, his eyes tracking Kenny as he handed the baby over. Lifting his head only at the neck, he then spotted Daisy and smiled.

"Daisy," Luke called out. "You're here."

"I got the SOS, but it looks like you delivered the baby."

"I did," he said proudly, sitting up. "Which means I get to name her."

"It's a girl?"

"Yeah, Sis, it's a girl," Archer said, sounding weary.

Daisy sobbed and looked at a sleeping Erica. "Is she okay?"

"Yeah. Luke has her and the baby sorted, but it was a long labour. Heidi is on the other side of the island with another mother. There was no way we were risking her coming in this storm. Jason is on his way to Heidi and will bring her here when it's safe."

"I'm so happy they're both doing okay. Are you okay?" Daisy asked.

"I'm a fucking father, Daiz."

The five boys laughed at his statement, now sitting on tea chests, kicking their feet. They seemed to have rallied. Kenny had joined them.

"Sorry, lads," Archer said, grimacing and looking down at his daughter.

Luke staggered to his feet and came over to hug Daisy. She cuddled him close.

"Well done, brother. What is her name?"

Luke looked to Archer and said, "Isobel."

Archer nodded and cooed her name.

"Beautiful," Daisy said.

"Hey, Daisy," Erica said quietly. "Want to meet your niece?"

"Yeah," Daisy said, grinning as she came to sit on the other side of Erica.

Daisy and Archer acted like book ends, keeping her in a sitting position. She was covered up with jumpers and coats that looked like they were from another era.

Daisy took Isobel into her arms and stroked the soft skin between her eyebrows. As she scanned her face and held her tight.

Daisy thought it was time Imelda Turner came home to Copper Island.

***

Thank you for reading Lipstick Kiss, the third book in *The Turners of Copper Island* series. I can't tell you how happy it makes me you spent the time reading it. The final book in the series is Electric Kiss, and find out about Daisy Turner.

If this series is your type of story, then check out Cynthia's story in instalments through my website while you wait. If you want to keep up to date with my future releases, sales, and giveaways, click HERE for my newsletter.

READER MESSAGE

Luke and Freya's story in Lipstick Kiss was so great to write. I fell in love with these two as I do with all my characters. Their dilemma over spoiling their close friendship to becoming lovers is a hard one for both of them. Especially living on a small island.

Check out Electric Kiss, the final book if you want to continue with this series.

If you get time, a rating or review would be amazing.

Want to keep up to date with my news? Then click HERE to subscribe to my newsletters. All news goes to email subscribers first.

Take care

Grace

You can find me online, search for GraceHarperBooks

ABOUT THE AUTHOR

I was born and raised in Wales, in a sleepy town just outside Cardiff. Developing a love of stationery at a very early age, I still can't pass a pen shop without nipping in for a quick look around.

Writing and publishing since 2012, I have many books in my back catalogue, all in the Romance genre. They range from Rock Star Romance to Small Town Romance to Family Sagas. Be warned, the stories have a steamy heat level!

In a nutshell?
21st Century Romance—Writing about understated powerful women. Understated love stories with a powerful message, each and every time.

ALSO BY GRACE HARPER
THE TURNERS OF COPPER ISLAND SERIES

The Turners are coming home and they're looking for love.

Reckless Kiss ~ Stolen Kiss ~ Lipstick Kiss ~ Electric Kiss ~ The Turners of Copper Island – Cynthia's Story

THE DEVOTED MEN SERIES

Three men, two brothers and their best friend find love in the most unexpected places. They are only looking to marry once and forever.
Charming Olivia ~ Loving Lilly ~ Tempting Angie

THE THIS LOVE SERIES

A rockstar romance spanning the years. A woman coming to terms with survivor's guilt and a man who will never give up on her.
THIS LOVE ~ THIS LOVE ALWAYS ~ THIS LOVE FOREVER ~ FIVE CHANCES

THE RED & BLACK SERIES

A record label series. Each of the record label owners and senior staff have their story told. Intrigue, revenge, rival record labels, and a whole lotta heat.
Charcoal Notes ~ Crimson Melodies ~ raven acoustics ~ cardinal lyrics ~ Onyx Keys ~ Vermillion Chords ~ Inky Rhapsodies ~ Magenta Symphonies ~ White Wedding

THE TALBOT GIRLS NOVELLAS

FESTIVE, SMALL-TOWN NOVELLAS TO WARM YOUR HEART.

Stranded at New Year ~ His Christmas Surprise ~ Under the Mistletoe ~ Snowflakes at Dawn ~ A Holiday Wish

STANDALONE NOVELS
THE STRANGER'S VOICE ~ HOLLYWOOD SPOTLIGHT ~ THE GIRL UPSTAIRS ~ FASHION ~ SERENADE

Sign up to my email list HERE

ACKNOWLEDGMENTS

My husband of over two decades is my ever love. Each story I write has a little bit of him in the hero.

Many people have supported me over the years with my novel writing. They should all be mentioned in every book as they shaped the writer I am today. I am thankful that I have a team behind me who keep me straight and make me laugh.

Not everyone helps on every book, but there are still there, cheerleading from the sidelines.

No one will love my characters as much as I do, but when I see a review that accurately says what I feel when I write about them, it is the most satisfying feeling in the world.

I am grateful to my readers. May you keep enjoying my books.

I also want the thank the makers of *Maltesers*. Without them, these books would not be published.

Printed in Great Britain
by Amazon